*For the Sharp family—Anne, Sandy, Katherine, and Wilson.
With love and gratitude.*

ASHLEY FARLEY

WHERE LIGHT LINGERS

Soul Seekers

Soul Seekers

Return to Marsh Hollow

Where Light lingers

When Sparks Fly

Cupid's Countdown

Messy Under the Mistletoe

Sandy Island

Southern Discomfort

Beneath the Carolina Sun

Southern Simmer

Marsh Point

Long Journey Home

Echoes of the Past

Songbird's Second Chance

Heart of Lowcountry

After the Storm

Scent of Magnolia

Virginia Vineyards

Love Child

Blind Love

Forbidden Love

Love and War

Palmetto Island

Muddy Bottom

Change of Tides

Lowcountry on My Mind

Sail Away

Hope Springs Series

Dream Big, Stella!

Show Me the Way

Mistletoe and Wedding Bells

Matters of the Heart

Road to New Beginnings

Stand Alone

On My Terms

Tangled in Ivy

Lies that Bind

Life on Loan

Only One Life

Home for Wounded Hearts

Nell and Lady

Sweet Tea Tuesdays

Saving Ben

Sweeney Sisters Series

Saturdays at Sweeney's

Tangle of Strings

Boots and Bedlam

Lowcountry Stranger

One

I've never felt so alone in a room full of people. And that's saying something, coming from someone used to lecturing five days a week to a hundred distracted students. But no one prepares you for this kind of silence—the kind that follows a eulogy, thick with memory and regret.

Half the town has turned out for my mother's memorial service. Alongside Flossie's many friends, I spot her attorney, financial planner, and hair stylist. In the far corner of the room, my father's old golf partners and fishing buddies huddle together as though waiting out a storm.

Flossie's friends from garden club, bridge club, and her church circle were always gracious about visiting during her illness. They brought food and flowers, stayed for short visits, and cast pitiful glances my way when Flossie repeated the same questions over and over again. Those visits slowed in recent months, as her mind began its final, rapid unraveling. Now they line up to pay their respects in the fellowship hall, engulfing me in warm hugs, their voices soft with nostalgia.

Your mama didn't just light up this block. She lit up the entire town.

There'll never be another Flossie.
She had a way of making everybody feel like family.
That garden of hers? It was a masterpiece.
Oh, we're going to miss her something fierce.

My gaze lands on a young woman I don't recognize. She has the purest face, a mop of white-blonde curls, and eyes so crystal clear they seem to glow. Our eyes meet, and a flicker passes between us, sending a jolt through me. There's something eerily familiar about her. Maybe she's one of my students? I glance away for just a second. When I look back, she's gone. An odd hollowness settles in my chest, like I've missed something important without knowing what it was. Not fear exactly—but a strange, wistful ache. A thread left dangling. A question unanswered.

I shrug it off. I'm overly emotional today.

My friends are here—Mary Beth, Lisa, Georgia. Not Janey. I saw her earlier in the church. But she's an obstetrician. She likely rushed off to deliver some lucky young woman's baby.

The five of us traveled in a pack from kindergarten through high school graduation—thick as honeysuckle on a porch railing. There were birthday parties with handmade cakes and scavenger hunts. Shopping trips on the Square during our awkward middle school years, trying on too much makeup and too-tight jeans. Sneaking into fraternity parties at Ole Miss when we were seniors in high school, bold with fake IDs and borrowed confidence.

We remained close through college, standing up in each other's weddings in pastel gowns and cemented updos. But then they started having babies, and I couldn't conceive. Being around them became intolerable, their talk of potty training and backyard barbecues painful reminders of my failures. After my divorce, I pulled away entirely. It wasn't just the babies or the husbands or the joyful chaos of their lives—it was the ache of what I'd lost, and what I never really had to begin with.

The three of them trade their fondest Flossie stories now. Everyone has always called my mother Flossie—even when we were kids.

"Mrs. Aldridge was my mother-in-law," she used to say when someone made the dreaded mistake of using her married name. "Heaven knows I don't want to be confused with that battle-ax—God rest her soul."

We laugh, remembering the night she piled us into her station wagon, in our pajamas, for a midnight run to the Krispy Kreme in Memphis. How she taught us to apply eyeliner with a gentle hand. How she let us sip champagne at her New Year's Eve parties—provided we handed over our car keys. How she once drove us to Nashville to see the Indigo Girls on a whim, blasting Fleetwood Mac the whole way. How she made everyone feel like her favorite—and somehow, we all believed we were.

I walk my friends to the side exit. Each one kisses the air beside my cheek in parting, but none suggest we get together soon. When I turn back around, the room has emptied. No one's in sight as I cross through the fellowship hall toward the sanctuary, but I can't shake the uneasy feeling that I'm not alone. That someone is watching me.

Retrieving Mom's urn from the church altar, I hurry out to my dusty blue 1984 Land Cruiser. Bluebell was already vintage when Dad gave her to me for my sixteenth birthday. I've repainted the exterior, rebuilt the engine, and reworked the white leather upholstery more times than I can count, but I still can't bring myself to part with her.

I buckle Mom into the passenger side. I'd chosen a blue and white delft ginger jar for her remains—classic and elegant, more my taste than hers. But when it turned out to be unavailable, the funeral home folks put her ashes in a squatty purple jug that looks like someone's first attempt at pottery class. When the director saw my face, he offered to transfer her to something more appropriate. But I declined. I didn't want to unsettle her. And honestly? The more I look at it, the more I think Flossie would've loved the color.

Bluebell's AC gave out about a decade ago and never came back to life. This weekend marks the beginning of summer, but today's weather is still spring-like, low humidity with temperatures in the seventies. I roll down the windows and let the jasmine-sweet air pour in as we make the short drive home —me and Flossie, one last ride together.

Rosa has changed out of her funeral dress and is in the kitchen waiting for us when we arrive. She engulfs me in a hug so tight the urn digs into my rib cage. She's a strong woman for someone so tiny.

"Bless your heart," she murmurs. "First your daddy, and now your mama. Both so young. Gone before their time. And you—"

"Am now an orphan," I say into her chest, the words muffled and bitter.

She pulls back to look at me, her eyes wet. "I just wish you had a sibling."

"Well, I don't," I snap. "Obviously."

"Let me see this." She takes the purple contraption from me and holds it up to the light, squinting at it like it might confess something. "Your mama is not happy in here."

My heart sinks. I gave Flossie everything I had these past three years. And now . . . I don't know how to stop caring, even when there's nothing left I can do.

I offer a sad smile. "She's definitely on the verge of a claustrophobic meltdown. Any thoughts on where I should scatter her ashes?"

The lines in Rosa's forehead deepen. "The mountains? The ocean? Maybe the Grand Canyon?"

I cut my eyes at her. "Seriously, Rosa? Flossie never went to the Grand Canyon. It needs to be somewhere meaningful, her special place. Like her garden."

Rosa lets out a humph. "You'd have to tame the jungle out there first. She'd roll over in that purple jug if she saw it now. Weeds taller than my knees. That fountain full of mosquito babies. And not a bloom in sight. Your mama would want her garden pretty again."

A pang of guilt grips my chest. I let her garden grow wild. "I'm aware."

I take the urn from her and head down the center hallway toward the living room. She trails behind, watching as I place it in the center of the mantel between two heavy brass candlesticks, each holding a creamy taper Flossie never lit. I turn the urn one way and another. But there's no good side. It's just plain ugly.

The doorbell lets out a cascading chime, like wind through crystal. "I'll get it," Rosa says, already scurrying off.

"Tell them to go away," I call after her, loud enough for whoever's at the door to hear me. "I'm not accepting company."

Murmured voices in the hallway at the front of the house are followed by the appearance of two uniformed men. The embroidered patches on their gray shirts read *CareFirst Home Solutions*.

The older one removes his hat and nods. "Afternoon, ma'am." He glances at his clipboard. "We're here for the medical equipment—hospital bed, bedside commode, toilet, oxygen, walker . . ."

"Seriously?" I snap. "My mother's service ended less than two hours ago. I didn't call you. How did you even know she'd died? Did you read her obituary in the newspaper?"

He shifts uncomfortably. "I'm sorry, ma'am. The pickup

order came through this morning. I don't know who placed it."

"I did," Rosa says, stepping forward. She sweeps a hand at the room. "Help yourselves, gentlemen."

I pull her into the hallway, lowering my voice. "You certainly didn't waste any time."

"What's the point of keeping all this equipment lying around? It'll only serve as a reminder."

My brow lifts. "A reminder? Of my mother? Am I supposed to erase all evidence of her now that she's dead?"

"Of course not, Selwyn," she says, gently. "A reminder of her illness. Of the heartache these past few years have brought."

"As if I could forget," I murmur, watching the men wheel out the hospital bed, the quiet scrape of rubber wheels against hardwood.

Within minutes, the hospital room is transformed back into a living room. Nothing remains but Mom's silk drapes and the patterned wool carpet, its colors faded around the rectangle where the bed sat for six long years.

"What did we do with the sofa and chairs that were in here?" I ask Rosa.

"Miss Flossie and I dragged them out to the garage. Remember?"

I nod, even though I have no recollection of it. Much of the last six years is a blur.

"Why don't you ask these men to move the furniture back while they're here?" Rosa suggests.

"Good idea." I return to the kitchen where I left my purse, retrieving two twenty-dollar bills from my wallet.

When the men give me the paperwork to sign, I hold up the cash between two fingers. "I've got a sofa and two chairs in the garage I'd like to bring back inside. Any chance you can help me?"

"Sorry, ma'am," the older man says, shaking his head. "It's Friday afternoon before a holiday weekend. We're on a tight schedule."

The younger man eyes the twenties, then elbows his co-worker in the ribs. "Come on, Carl. We can spare a few extra minutes."

Carl exhales an annoyed sigh. "All right. But let's get to it."

"Follow me." I lead them through the kitchen, out the back door, across the porch, and down the overgrown garden path to the garage. Sliding open the doors, we're greeted by the smells of mildew and motor oil. As we make our way past Flossie's old yard tools and stacked planters, a sudden crash sounds from overhead.

I stop in my tracks. "What was that?"

The younger man glances up at the beamed ceiling. "I'm not sure. What's up there?"

I follow his gaze. "An apartment. But nobody's been up there in years." I shrug. "It's probably just squirrels. I'll have my lawn crew check it out next week."

We continue to the back of the garage, where the furniture is covered in sheets like forgotten ghosts, waiting to be remembered. I lift the corner of the sofa sheet and gasp. The once-cheerful buttery-yellow fabric is now mottled with mold. I yank the sheets off the chairs to find them in the same condition.

Flossie would have a conniption.

I haven't cried since she drew her last breath. I've been numb, a zombie moving through the motions of planning the funeral. But now, staring at the mold blooming like bruises on the yellow fabric, I feel the sting rise behind my eyes.

This is what grief looks like. Not the casseroles. Not the sympathy cards. Something once beautiful, left too long to rot.

"Looks like I wasted your time," I say, letting the sheet fall back into place. "These belong in the dump."

"I'm sorry, ma'am," the young man says, frowning as he hands me back the money.

I shake my head. "You keep it. Thanks for your willingness to help. Have a nice weekend."

Carl walks ahead to the truck, but the younger guy lingers, helping me close the heavy garage doors.

"I have a pickup truck," he says. "If you want, I can come back sometime and haul the furniture to the dump. Anything else you might want to get rid of too."

"Good to know. Leave me your number."

"I do odd jobs on the side." He hands me his business card. Across the top, printed in bold letters, it reads: *Jack of All Trades.* Below that—his name, Jack Brunson, followed by his number.

I can't help but smile. "Cute. I'll remember that," I say, slipping the card into my dress pocket.

As I traipse back through the garden, my heels sinking into the overgrown path, I glance around at the tangle of weeds and wilted blooms. It's a mess out here—just like my life. The long holiday weekend looms ahead. Summer school doesn't start until Tuesday. For the first time in years, I have no family waiting inside. No one left to take care of. And I've never felt so lost.

Two

As I push open the back door, Rosa's humming reaches me—soft and steady, the opening notes of "How Great Thou Art." It was Flossie's favorite. Her request. She chose it herself for her funeral. Now the tune floats through the house like a benediction. I follow it into the living room where I find her on a step stool, dusting the bookshelves—quietly tending to the things Mama left behind, just as she always has.

Sensing me in the entryway, she glances over her shoulder, eyes fixed on the space behind me. "Well? Where's the furniture?"

"In the garage. Ruined—covered in mold. What was Flossie thinking, storing it in an unconditioned space? She, of all people, should've known better."

"She wasn't thinking clearly," Rosa says softly.

The truth in her offhand comment hangs in the air between us. I can't remember a time when my mother *was* thinking clearly. When I moved home to help take care of Dad, I started noticing things—subtle slips, odd moments. Who knows how long the disease had been creeping in.

I circle the room, contemplating the empty space. "I could bring over some of my furniture from storage," I say. "But I'm not sure it would work with Flossie's color palette."

A wistful smile spreads across her lips. "Miss Flossie sure did love her some color."

"That's an understatement. This house is a kaleidoscope. Yellow living room. Pink dining room. Baby blue bedroom. The color-drenched whimsical wallpapers in the bathrooms. Dad's study escaped, but only because of the wood paneling."

"Robin's egg blue," Rosa says, stepping down off the stool.

I arch an eyebrow. "Excuse me? Robin's egg who?"

"Miss Flossie's bedroom is robin's egg blue," she says. "Her favorite color."

"I stand corrected," I say, a wave of weariness settling over me. I start toward the stairs. "I'm going up to change. If you leave before I come back down, have a nice weekend."

"You do the same," she calls after me. "And try to get some rest."

I'm halfway up the stairs when I hear her whistling. Retracing my steps, I stand in the arched doorway watching her waltz around the room with her feather duster. "How can you be so happy when Flossie's memorial service was today?"

Rosa's face softens as she lowers her feather duster. "I'm not happy, Selwyn. I'm *relieved* for her. Your mama is finally free of that awful disease that was eating up her brain. She can think straight again. She's up in heaven right now, challenging your father on a crossword puzzle."

I can't help but smile. My parents had raging battles over the newspaper's daily crossword. "I can see them now, seated at a kitchen table on a cloud. Drinking coffee and arguing about the puzzle." *Do they even have coffee in heaven?*

Tucking her duster under her arm, Rosa walks over to me,

taking my hands in hers. "Funerals are for mourning, Selwyn. It's natural to feel sad. But you know how much Miss Flossie despised self-pity. She wouldn't want you to wallow. Things need to get back to normal around here."

"Normal?" I laugh, but there's no humor in it. "Nothing will ever be normal without my parents."

"Sure it will. Maybe not the same kind of normal—but a new kind. It'll come."

I pull my hands free. "For six years, I've been nursing my parents. I have no clue how to move on, Rosa."

"Well . . ." Rosa pauses, thoughtful. "You can start by inviting some of your friends over."

"My friends are busy raising kids. I have nothing in common with any of them."

"Then make some new friends! Bring some life and laughter back into this house."

I glare at her. "Forgive me if I don't feel like laughing."

"You will. In time. One day you'll meet a nice man, maybe remarry. He might have children of his own. Or maybe you'll adopt. Or foster." She waves the duster around in the air. "Fill this house with love again."

"You mean, fill this house with more people for me to take care of." Turning away, I trudge up the stairs to my room.

I wait until I hear the back door shut and the sound of Rosa's car pulling out of the driveway before venturing back down-stairs. I thought I wanted to be alone, but now that I am, I have no idea what to do with myself. I've spent six years of Friday nights in this house. But I was never alone. I was always with Flossie. She was good company, right until the end. Watching movies with her could test my patience—she'd lose track of the characters, ask what was going on, then ask again, sometimes three times in the same scene. And yet, when the credits rolled, she always cried. Happy ending, sad ending—it didn't matter. Even if she couldn't recall the plot, she still felt the weight of it. The emotion stayed, even when the story slipped away.

Her condition was rapidly deteriorating, and I was bracing for a rough road ahead—long, hard, cruel—when she came down with the flu, which quickly turned into pneumonia. As much as I hated watching her die, a part of me now realizes we were both spared the worst of her disease.

I roam through the empty rooms, studying the photographs of the family of three who once lived here.

There we are on Easter—posed in front of the azaleas, my father in his seersucker suit, Flossie radiant in a wide-brimmed hat, one arm wrapped around an adolescent me.

And a beach trip from the same decade—sunburned noses, windblown hair, Flossie's sunglasses perched crooked on her face as she laughs at something I can't remember.

My high school graduation—my smile uncertain, Dad's hand firm on my shoulder, and Flossie dabbing her eyes behind the camera.

We look happy. We look real. We look like people I almost remember.

I never regretted being an only child. Even when I was the soul caregiver. As with most only children, my parents raised me to be an adult by the time I was ten. They never talked down to me, never softened the truth. We didn't do baby talk or bedtime stories—we had dinner table debates and heated discussions about current events, even when I was too young to fully understand them. They expected more of me, earlier. And I rose to meet them, eager to prove I was worthy of their attention. Being their only child meant I got all of it—every ounce of their love but also their worry, their expectations, their disappointments.

I stand in front of the fireplace, staring at the purple urn. I was stunned when I opened the file marked *Funeral Instructions* after Flossie's death and discovered she wanted to be cremated. I had always assumed she'd be buried beside Dad at St. Peter's Cemetery. Tucked inside the file was a handwritten letter—dated ten years ago.

My darling Selwyn,

You know how much I deplore doing anything by the book. So why should death be any different? For most of my life, I stood beside your father, through thick and thin. But I've decided to go out on my own in the afterlife. Cremate me! And spread my ashes over a place of your choosing. Somewhere beautiful. Somewhere fragrant. You'll know it when you find it.

My dying wish,
Flossie

Her comment—*through thick and thin*—makes me wonder if they were having marital problems. They always seemed so perfect together, the quintessential couple. They finished each other's sentences and always knew what the other was thinking. Although there was a period when they seemed to argue a lot—right around the time I graduated from college. I mean this affectionately, but my father was a scoundrel—charming, secretive, and just slippery enough to get away with things. He had that half smile that could smooth over a lie before it ever reached his lips. If he'd had an affair, Flossie would've found out about it. Of course, she would've chosen grace over drama. That was her way.

I'm sitting at my father's mahogany desk when I notice a

photograph—faded and curling at the edges—tucked beneath the leather border of his blotter. It's a little girl, no older than five. Chubby cheeks. A halo of white-blonde curls. She's squinting into the sun, her mouth caught halfway between a smile and a pout. I lean closer, heart thudding. This isn't me. I have my mother's deep-chestnut waves. I've never seen this photo. Never seen this child. Before I can take it all in, a knock at the back door cuts through the silence.

Slipping the photo back under the blotter's border, I get up and hurry to the kitchen. I'm surprised to see Janey standing in the doorway, a shopping bag from Chicory Market in one hand and a giant bouquet of flowers in the other.

She starts chattering the minute I enter the room. "I'm sorry I missed you at the funeral. I had to sneak out early to deliver a baby. The service was lovely, Sel. Your mama would've approved."

Janey is as pretty as ever—her perky blonde ponytail dancing around her shoulders. She hasn't changed a bit. We were best friends in high school, closer than the others. And even now, I feel a connection with her that never really faded. If not for her career, we would probably see each other more often. Unlike the others, she's careful not to talk too much about her son around me. I've often wondered why she stopped at one child. If that was by choice or design.

"I brought you dinner." She sets the bag on the counter and hands me the bouquet of mixed spring flowers—sweet pea, lisianthus, stock, foxglove, and snapdragon. "Aren't they just gorgeous? My friend Katherine Webb is a flower farmer out at the Farmstead. Her parents, Ann and Sandy Sharp, are wonderful people. They have a stunning wedding venue, if you ever . . ."

Her voice trails off.

An awkward silence blooms between us—thick with everything neither of us says. I'm not planning a wedding.

Not for me. Not for a daughter. And if I ever get married again, it won't be at a venue like the Farmstead. It'll be barefoot on a beach somewhere far away, just me, my man, and the breeze.

Finally, Janey clears her throat. "Anyway, the flowers reminded me of Flossie. I used to love digging in her garden."

I laugh at the memory. "She never allowed anyone to work in her garden except you. Not even me."

"Those were special times. I dearly loved her," Janey says, her eyes glistening with unshed tears.

She crosses the kitchen to the cabinet where Flossie used to keep her vases—I'm surprised she remembers. With practiced ease, she pulls out a simple tall glass one, fills it with water, and begins arranging the flowers, her hands moving with quiet familiarity.

When she finishes fussing with the flowers, she looks up at me. "Was it terrible? The Alzheimer's? The personality changes for some are devastating."

I shake my head. "She had little personality change. Flossie's was mostly just memory. In a way, I think we were spared. But I have a feeling the situation was about to get much worse."

I open the refrigerator door and take out a bottle of sauvignon blanc. "Would you like a glass of wine?"

She waves her hand. "I can't. I'm on call."

I return the wine to the refrigerator and remove a pitcher of Rosa's sweet sun tea. "How about tea?"

Janey smiles but shakes her head. "I really can't stay. I don't want to intrude."

Intrude on what? Dinner preparations for my nonexistent family?

I nod and force a smile, even though every part of me wants to say, *Please. Stay.*

"Will you continue to live in the house?"

Irritation creeps into my voice. "Why wouldn't I? Because it's a big house, and there's only me?"

Janey appears wounded. "Not at all. This is your home. I just meant . . . it's a lot to keep up. I wasn't sure if . . . financially . . ." She trails off, eyes glancing nervously toward the door. "Never mind. It's none of my business anyway. I just wanted to bring you some dinner and make sure you're all right."

I soften, ashamed of my harsh tone. "Thanks. I didn't mean to jump down your throat. I haven't spoken to the estate attorney yet. You remember Walter—Dad's law partner. I assume he would've said something if there's a money problem."

"I'm sure everything is fine. I miss you, Sel." Janey's voice is quiet. "You've been gone a long time—even when you were right here."

Her words land like a stone in my chest. She's not wrong. I've been physically present but emotionally somewhere else— lost in caretaking, in grief, in silence.

I look down, not trusting myself to speak. Finally, I manage a weak smile. "I miss you too."

She kisses my cheek and waves as she hurries out the back door.

From the doorway, I watch Janey leave in her Mercedes convertible. Not a mommy car but the kind a confident, professional woman drives.

She's right. While the same brown-eyed girl stares back at me from the mirror every morning, I haven't felt like myself in . . . I don't even know when. Since before the divorce. What happened to that girl? The fun-loving one who hosted book club, went to author signings, threw themed dinner parties. The athletic one who swam laps, ran five miles before breakfast, played tennis every Saturday.

My gaze travels across the driveway. The girl who used to pile her friends into her Land Cruiser and head to Gulfport for the weekend—wind in her hair, a mixtape in the cassette deck, not a care in the world.

I sigh as I close the back door, leaning against it. Life happened to that girl. She realized she would never have children. Became alienated from her friends. Lost both parents in six years.

That girl needs to find some new meaning in her life—if it's not already too late.

Three

Grief makes the simplest tasks feel impossible. I've been staring at the same thank-you note for ten minutes, coffee gone cold, when I catch a flicker of movement at the back door. A shadow—or maybe just my imagination. I turn around. No one's there.

Minutes later, the front doorbell rings. That explains it— another casserole-bearing neighbor. But why are they calling so early on a Saturday morning? Don't they have any common decency?

I consider ignoring them, but whoever it is went to a lot of trouble. It's not their fault I'm in a bad mood.

As I round the corner from the kitchen into the hallway, I catch a man's face through the side window. He's staring right at me. He looks oddly familiar—like someone I once knew but haven't seen in a long time. I squint. Is that Griffin? His hairline has receded, and crow's feet now gather at the corner of his gray eyes, but he's still as handsome as ever.

I swing open the door. "Griffin! This is a surprise."

A slow smile spreads across his full lips. "Hey, Selwyn. I'm so sorry about Flossie. She was a character—always good for a laugh." He chuckles. "Although I admit I was more than a little afraid of her. Remember that time she caught me sneaking out of your bedroom late at night?"

I smile. "How could I forget? She sent you home with chocolate chip cookies, but even though we were only studying, she grounded me for two weeks." I raise my voice in a screech imitation. "'You should know better, Selwyn. Proper young women don't entertain men in their bedrooms.'"

Griffin laughs. "Sounds just like her."

My smile fades. "What're you doing here? I thought you lived in Atlanta."

"I do . . . I did. I'm getting a divorce and decided to move back. I'm a real estate agent. I thought you might be putting the house on the market soon and figured I'd reach out."

Irritation prickles my skin. "Because this house is too big for poor little me to manage on my own?"

He flinches at my tone. "I didn't mean to offend you, Selwyn. I heard you were divorced. That you don't have any children. I thought maybe you'd be looking for something . . . smaller."

I shake my head slowly, disappointed but not surprised. "Same old opportunistic Griffin. You haven't changed a bit."

His brow furrows. "What's that supposed to mean?"

"So, you've forgotten? Well, let me refresh your memory. You went off to college in August. By September, you had a new girlfriend."

His jaw drops. "We agreed to see other people, Selwyn."

"We didn't agree, Griffin. You made that decision for us. *Seeing other people* usually implies we're still seeing each other too. But you brought home your blonde bombshell for Christmas—paraded her in front of me at every party. Next thing I know, you two are married. Never mind all the forever plans we made for our future."

Griffin stiffens. "I see I caught you at a bad time. Maybe it's too soon."

Heat rises in my cheeks. "You think? We haven't seen each other in decades, and you show up on my doorstep the day after my mother's memorial service, asking if I want to sell my family's home." I pause to catch my breath. "*Too soon* is an understatement. *Presumptuous* is a more fitting description. Or *callous*, depending on how you look at it."

"I'm sorry for upsetting you, Selwyn. Call me if you change your mind about the house," he says, pressing a business card in my palm.

"I won't be needing this." My fingers tremble as I tear the card into tiny pieces, watching him walk down the sidewalk to his Yukon parked at the curb.

He doesn't look back as he drives away.

I slam the door and collapse against it, inhaling and exhaling slowly to settle my racing heart. Slumped against the front door, I can see through the entryway into the living room. The purple jug sits on the mantel where I left it, smug in its silence. "So, I may have overreacted," I say to the urn.

She doesn't respond, of course. Flossie always knew when to hold her tongue.

Pushing off the door, I walk into the living room and approach the mantel. "I need to do something with your remains soon. I can't have you watching my every move."

I turn away from the mantel. "And as for you, Griffin McRae, I'll show you, and everyone else in this town, that I can take care of this house."

I wrinkle my nose and wave a hand in front of my face. "We'll start by letting in some fresh air. This place reeks of death."

I march from room to room, pulling back the drapes and throwing open the windows. From Dad's study at the back of the house, I pause to look out at the overgrown garden. For the neighbors' sake, I need to do something with this eyesore.

I change into old clothes, grab a pair of pruning shears from the garage, and go to war with the yard. I don't know the difference between weeds and plants, so I cut everything in any shade of green. Three hours later, I've barely made a dent—despite the mountain of bagged debris waiting at the curb.

I'm plucking soggy leaves from the fountain basin when I get an eerie sense that someone is watching me. My eyes scan the house, then the yard, finally landing on the second-story window of the garage apartment. There's a glint, a glimmer of movement. Is someone there? Or is it just my imagination—the sun catching the glass at just the right angle?

Uneasy, I return the pruning shears and head inside.

As I step into the kitchen, something flutters past my face with a rush of air and panic. A bird—flailing, frenzied—circles the room, its wings beating wildly as it slams against the window glass, desperate to escape.

I duck instinctively, covering my face with my arm. The windows! I left them open while I was outside.

I go to the pantry, grab a broom, and fling open the back door. "Go!" I plead, chasing it from corner to corner. "Just go!"

After several tense laps around the room and one near miss with a glass-paned cabinet, the bird finally finds the open air and vanishes in a blur of feathers and freedom. I sag against the doorframe, heart still hammering. It's gone. But for a moment, it felt like the house itself had turned against me.

I take a breath, still gripping the broom. The silence settles in again, only now it feels different. The air is fresh. And for the first time in ages, the house feels cleaner, less like a tomb.

After closing all the windows, I take a long hot shower, towel dry my chin-length hair, and dress in loungewear. Not pajamas, not clothes, just the in-between uniform of someone who doesn't plan on leaving the house. Or doing much of anything, really.

Returning to the kitchen, I inspect the refrigerator's contents. There are plenty of casseroles to choose from. Macaroni and cheese. Chicken divan. Chicken and rice. The vegan lasagna Janey brought. But the heaviness in my heart extends to my gut, and I choose a glass of wine instead.

I sit down at the table with the abandoned list of thank-you notes and set to work. I write a handful before I hear the soft patter of rain on the windows—just after sunset. It starts as barely a whisper, but it's steady. Relentless. The kind of rain that settles in for the night.

I take my untouched glass of wine to Dad's study. As a child, I was forbidden to enter without an invitation. Truthfully, I never minded. The room has always felt . . . heavy. All that dark paneling, the looming bookshelves, the air thick with the scent of musty books. Even now, it presses in on me. Such a shame too. Tucked in the back corner of the house just off the porch, the room overlooks the yard through wide windows. It would make a lovely morning room or a cozy little den.

From the window, I watch the garden disappear into the storm. The boxwoods blur into one dark shape, and the fountain is nothing more than a shadow. I rest my forehead against the glass, cold and damp with condensation. My grief has no sharp edges anymore. Just weight.

Truthfully, I lost my mother a long time ago. She looked the same. She laughed the same. But her eyes were often blank, her face expressionless. Her mind was already gone. And somehow, knowing what was coming didn't make it hurt any less.

I turn away from the window and walk toward the living room—the hub of activity for my family. For our small town, really. It was Flossie's stage. Her laughter was the spotlight—

drawing people in, keeping them there. One of her friends at the memorial service had described her as *a colorful character in every way.* She was sometimes silly. Usually laughing. Always compassionate with a friend in need. But never judgmental. At least not with her friends. I wouldn't say she judged me, exactly. But she had high expectations for her only child. And I let her down. I never won an award. Never achieved anything that looked like success. Never even gave her a grandchild.

In fairness to me, I'm not sure I ever really knew what she wanted. She never said it outright—just riddles, metaphors, and half hints I could never quite decode. And now she's gone. I'll never get the chance to make her proud of me again.

And now it's just me. Alone in this empty house. An empty social schedule. An empty life.

A shiver dances down my arm, goosebumps rising like a warning. I can't shake the feeling someone's watching me. The hospital bed is gone, but Flossie still reigns from the mantel, lording over me from inside that purple jug.

Death didn't soften her presence. If anything, it sharpened it.

I turn my back on the purple jug and return to the kitchen. I open my day planner. Aside from my classes, the pages are blank. No parties. No weddings. Certainly no vacations. Just an ocean of white space.

Closing the planner, I lift my gaze to Flossie's prescription pill bottles lined up neatly in a row. I need to dispose of them, but how? If I throw them away, they could end up in the wrong person's hands.

I unscrew the cap on her painkillers and shake the contents out in my hand. Fifteen, maybe twenty pills. Powerful medicine. Enough to get the job done. To end this pitiful existence. I stare at the little blue pills, the weight of them settling into my skin. *I wonder what heaven is like.* But if I take these, I won't get there. Not according to the Bible.

The doorbell startles me, and I nearly drop the pills. Who could be out in this weather? Certainly not a neighbor delivering another casserole. I pour the pills back in the bottle, screw the lid on tight, and return it to the lineup of medications beside the refrigerator.

Heading down the hall, I open the front door to find a drenched pizza delivery guy standing on my stoop, the rain pouring in torrents behind him.

"Did you order a pizza?" he asks, his blue eyes peeking out from beneath the hood of his yellow rain jacket.

I shake my head. "Sorry. Wrong house."

He checks the soggy paper in his hand. "One Hundred Willow Way?"

I frown. "Right address. But there must be some mistake. I'm the only one living here, and I didn't order a pizza."

He shrugs. "Okay, then. Have a nice night," he says, vanishing into the rain.

I lock the door behind him and return to the kitchen.

I'll take the prescriptions back to the pharmacy in the morning. They'll know how to dispose of them. Flossie is gone, and I don't want to be tempted again. But as I'm dropping the bottles into a plastic shopping bag, I notice the painkillers are missing. Frowning, I remove each bottle, one by one, checking the labels carefully. Not here.

I dig through the trash in case I tossed it in by accident on my way to the door. Still nothing. Strange.

That unsettling feeling creeps back in—like I'm not alone. Like someone is watching me.

I stare up at the ceiling. "Flossie? Are you haunting me? My words fall flat in the empty room. You can stop playing tricks on me. It's not funny."

I pour the untouched wine down the drain, make a cup of

lavender tea, and go upstairs to my bedroom. Standing by the window, I sip slowly and watch raindrops slide down the glass in shimmering trails.

"I could use some guidance, God. I nursed my parents through their illnesses. Now that they're gone, what am I supposed to do with myself?"

The words hang in the quiet, but I keep going.

"I sense a pull toward you, but I don't think it's my time to die. I feel like there's something left for me here. A purpose. A calling."

I wrap my hands tighter around the mug, warming my fingers.

"I'm forty-one years old, and my real life's work hasn't even begun. But what is it, Lord? Is it teaching? Is it my students?"

I used to think it was. I loved the exchange of ideas, the way a single line from Faulkner or Welty could crack open something real in a student's heart. But lately, it's harder to break through. They're distracted—more interested in their phones than the stories we're supposed to be unpacking together. Most days, I leave campus wondering if I'm reaching anyone at all.

Still . . . every once in a while, one of them looks up with eyes lit, really getting something. And for a brief second, it feels like enough. But is that all there is? Is that what I'm meant to do with the rest of my life?

I let out a quiet sigh. "As for romance, I'm not interested —unless the right man falls into my lap." A faint smile tugs at my lips. "Okay, maybe I am. A little. Isn't everyone who's single looking for love?"

My smile slips as the truth presses in again—that I don't know who I am without someone to care for, some clear path forward. "Please, Lord. Just show me the way."

Four

I'm out of my depth in the garden center. I barely know a daisy from a dandelion. I'm here because . . . I'm honestly not sure why I'm here. Being outside feels better than being in that house—with its silence and shadows and that purple jug staring at me from the mantel.

I woke up on the wrong side of the bed, and it's been downhill ever since. I can't stop thinking about what almost happened last night. I want to believe it was just a moment of desperation—a fleeting panic about the future. But deep down, I know it was more than that. I *am* unhappy. Unfulfilled. Afraid. And the idea of ending my life didn't feel as far-fetched as it should have. Whether it's the so-called easy way out, it seemed like it at that moment. But that's not who I am.

I don't judge anyone who's made a different choice. I just know I couldn't do that to the people who love me. No matter how miserable I feel, I won't leave that kind of scar on my family. I won't tarnish my parents' legacy with something I can't take back.

And so—I'm here. Still here. Wandering aimlessly through rows of brightly colored blooms.

I'm ashamed to admit, I don't know the difference between perennials and annuals. Me, Selwyn Aldridge—daughter of Oxford's Garden Queen. The only plant I recognize in the whole garden center is an azalea over in the blooming shrubs section. But that's no big deal. Every Southern girl knows azaleas.

I'm about to give up and go home when a voice behind me, smooth as honey, says, "You look like you could use some help."

I turn to find one of the most strikingly beautiful women I've ever seen. Her unblemished skin glows softly, the color of cognac. Her green eyes are clear and sparkling, like polished emeralds. A crown of silver coils is tied atop her head with a large pink flower. She wears faded overalls under a green apron, the pockets overflowing with clippers, seed packets, and garden twine.

"Thanks, but I doubt you can give me the help I need," I grumble. "I'm in over my head. I'll either hire a landscape crew or pour concrete over the whole backyard."

She chuckles—a warm, delightful sound that draws a smile to my face despite my mood. "Don't give up just yet," she says. "Tell me about your project. I might be able to at least point you in the right direction."

"Well . . . you see . . . I'm restoring my mother's garden. She died this week—" And to my horror, the tears come hot and fast, spilling over before I can stop them.

Everyone I've encountered over the past few days already knew about my mother's death. This is the first time I've said the words aloud. They land heavier than I expected—thick, final, undeniable. Saying them makes it real in a way that casseroles and sympathy cards never did.

"Oh, honey," she says, her fingers grazing my arm. "I'm so sorry. Had she been ill?"

I nod, biting my quivering lip as the tears stream like a river I didn't know I was holding back. "Alzheimer's."

She presses a tissue in my hand and gently pulls me out of the way of a passing throng of shoppers. Her hand moves in soft circles on my back until I compose myself.

"Tell me a little about Flossie's garden," she says in a voice like warm tea. "When you say you're restoring it, just how bad is it?"

"It's way overgrown, practically a jungle." I narrow my eyes at her. "Wait a minute. How do you know my mother's name? Have we met?"

"I don't believe we have." She offers her hand. "I'm Blossom."

"Blossom?" I scoff. "You can't be serious. What's your last name? Bouquet?"

She laughs, and despite myself, I take her hand. There's a warmth in her touch that wraps around me like morning light. For the first time in days, I feel like maybe I'm not falling apart.

"How long has it been since anyone tended the garden?" she asks.

I pause, thinking. "Flossie began neglecting it when my dad got sick—six years ago. She might have worked out there a little, but not like she used to." I let out a breath. "Yesterday, I went at it with a pair of pruning shears. I cut back as much as I could." I shrug. "Weeds. Plants. I'm not sure which was which."

"I'd be happy to take a look if you'd like. I can give you some pointers on how to get started." She gestures toward the exit.

"You mean now?" I ask.

She nods, a hint of mischief glinting in her eyes. "No time like the present!"

"Can you leave? Aren't you working here?" I glance at her apron.

She follows my gaze and chuckles. "This old thing? It's my garden apron." She leans in conspiratorially. "The youngsters who work here wouldn't be caught dead in something like this."

I survey the crowd. The other workers wear faded flannel shirts and ripped jeans. "I see that."

"Shall we?" she asks, already heading for the door.

I can't believe I'm inviting a total stranger named Blossom to my home. But honestly? She's the most fun I've had in years. And something tells me Flossie would approve. "Sure. Why not?" I say, smiling to myself as I follow her outside.

Blossom shields her eyes from the sun as she scans the parking lot. "I bet that cute vintage Land Cruiser is yours. Blue suits you, Selwyn."

I freeze mid-step. "Hold on. I don't remember telling you my name."

She flashes that easy smile over her shoulder.

And just like that, I'm trailing behind her—like someone who should know better but doesn't care.

I'm not surprised when she slides into the passenger seat. I'm so intrigued by this woman, I'm afraid to let her out of my sight for fear I might lose her. And something tells me she's holding some of the answers I'm searching for.

I don't ask how she'll get back to the garden center. I'll bring her if necessary.

Once we've left the parking lot, she asks, "Why are you resurrecting the garden if you have no interest in flowers?"

I narrow my eyes as I merge into traffic. "Good question. Lots of reasons, actually. Mainly for the neighbors' sake. The place is an eyesore."

"And?" Her raised eyebrow dares me to go deeper.

I lift my hands off the steering wheel, palms up like I'm surrendering to the universe. "I may sell the house. No one will make an offer in its current state."

"But you've lived there all your life. How could you sell your family's home?

I let out a slow breath. "I thought I could. I keep telling myself it's just a house. But it's not—*not really.*"

"Selling a house is one thing. Letting go of it? That's something else entirely."

I glance over at her. "How do you know so much about me?"

"It's my job." Before I can press her, she continues, "And your father? Did you lose him too?"

"Yeah. Three years ago. Cancer—the kind that takes everything from a person, piece by piece." I slow to a stop at a red light. "I was in the middle of divorcing my husband when Dad was diagnosed. Since my ex owned our house, I had to find somewhere to go. So, I moved back home to help take care of Dad. Not long after, I started noticing things weren't quite right with Flossie."

Blossom shakes her head. "You've really had a tough go. You never even had time to mourn him properly."

I tighten my grip on the steering wheel. "No, I guess I didn't." Flossie's memory was really slipping during Dad's final months. I took a leave of absence from the university that fall to help her cope. After he passed, she wandered around the house looking for him, forgetting that he'd died. Then she'd get irrationally angry, yelling at the photo of them on their honeymoon—the one he kept on his desk—accusing him of things that made little sense. I guess it was just the disease. Wasn't it?

As I pull into the driveway, Blossom peers out the window at the tangled yard.

If she's startled by the garden's disarray, she hides it well.

We climb out of the car, and she walks the edge of the garden, taking it in before offering her opinion.

"The garden has nice bones. The fountain just needs a little cleaning up. A power washer will take care of that. And the boxwood-lined paths need reshaping." She tilts her head, surveying the space. "But honestly, I'm not sure how much is worth salvaging. You'd have to wait weeks to see what comes up. And even then, it might not be something you love. Or it might not bloom at all."

"What're you suggesting?" I ask.

"That you start fresh—with the plants, at least. Choose the flowers you love, not the ones your mama did. It's your house now. You're the one who has to live with them." She kneels and plucks an errant weed growing between the bricks. "You did a great job of taking everything down to the ground, but I recommend scraping it clean and adding more condi-tioned soil. I know an excellent crew—I can have them give you an estimate if you'd like."

"I don't need an estimate as long as you trust them to do a good job."

"Very much so. It's already late in the blooming season, and we'll have to move fast. We can go back to the garden center in the morning and make our selections. The owner is a friend—she'll give us a discount. Then we'll get to planting."

"How long will that take? I'm teaching a summer school class starting on Tuesday."

"At least a couple of weeks. But I can work on it while you're in class."

"Do you charge by the hour?" I ask, imagining her still around come Labor Day.

She grins. "Oh, no. I'll do it for free. This isn't work for me. This is fun."

I scrunch up my nose. "I don't understand. Why would you do that when you don't even know me?"

"I know enough about you." She circles the fountain, running her hand along the rim. "It would really help to see photos of what it looked like in its prime—back when everything was blooming. That would give me a sense of the original design—the color palette and layering and style—formal, structured, or more cottage-like."

"Hmm. I'm sure Flossie has some photos on her phone. The question is, where *is* her phone? I haven't seen it in months. It's probably upstairs in her bedroom." I gesture toward the back door. "Come on in. I'll get you some tea while I look for it."

Blossom follows me into the kitchen. I'm reaching for the pitcher of Rosa's sun tea when I notice her heading straight to the cabinet where we keep the glasses. I say nothing. I tell myself it was just a good guess. Still, I can't shake the feeling there's more to her than meets the eye.

I find my mother's cell phone in her bedside table drawer —the battery dead, of course. I bring it back to the kitchen and plug it into my charger.

"It'll take a minute to charge," I say, sitting across from Blossom at the breakfast table, where a glass of tea awaits me.

Blossom folds her hands on the table. "That's fine. We'll talk flowers while we wait. You must have some favorites."

"I love daisies. They're so sweet and happy." A smile tugs at my lips as a faraway look crosses my face. "I insisted on having them in my bridal bouquet. Flossie nearly had a conniption. She'd already ordered these elaborate blooms and arranged them herself. She considered the daisy a highway flower, something you'd see growing in a ditch."

Blossom chuckles. "I'm with you, Selwyn. I love daisies too. They're tough, cheerful little things. They pop up where nothing else dares to grow, and they don't ask for much. Give them a little sun and a little room to breathe, and they'll bloom their hearts out."

I smile into my tea. "Flossie never understood that."

Blossom grins. "Well, I do. And I think it suits you just fine." She gives me a wink. "Mind if I call you Daisy?"

I laugh, caught off guard. "You can if you want. I've certainly been called worse. But why?"

"Because you strike me as a tough, cheerful little thing. You've been through the dark, pushed up through the cracks, and you're still blooming—whether or not you know it."

Her words settle over me like sunlight. I grab Flossie's phone, power it on, and scroll through the pics until I find a few of the garden.

I don't even realize I've been shifting my gaze toward the living room until Blossom asks, "What is so interesting behind me that's got your attention?"

I blink, surprised. "Oh. I guess subconsciously I've been looking at Flossie's urn."

I set the phone on the table. "She left a note asking me to spread her ashes somewhere beautiful and fragrant—a place of my choosing. She said I'd know it when I found it." I pause. "The request is weighing on me. I should be in no hurry, but for some reason, I feel like I'm racing the clock to get her settled."

Blossom doesn't hesitate. "I think you already know the place." Her voice is soft and steady. Like she's not just making a guess—she's sure.

I lower my head. "The garden makes sense. It's the logical place." I stare at the photo on Flossie's phone, her roses in full bloom. "I know what I said earlier about not selling the house. But what if I change my mind?" I glance toward the living room, where the purple jug waits. "If I scatter her ashes here . . . I'd have to leave her behind."

She places a warm hand over mine. "Ashes return to the earth, Daisy. But love settles in the heart and stays there. No matter where your feet land."

"That's lovely, Blossom. Thank you."

My mother lived in this house all her married life. It only seems fitting for her ashes to return to the earth here—not some far-off place with white sandy beaches that meant nothing to her. This was her home. Her roots are already here.

Five

I'm scrolling through my junk email and sipping coffee on Monday morning when I hear the low rumble of a truck engine, followed by the lively chatter of men speaking Spanish. Their voices rise above the quiet house—far too animated for a holiday, when the rest of the world is still in pajamas.

I shut my laptop, pour the dregs of my coffee down the sink, and step outside. Blossom has set up a card table beside a sky-blue mini school bus and is handing out steaming cups of coffee and foil-wrapped breakfast sandwiches.

"How did you pull this off on such short notice—on a holiday Monday, no less?" I call to her from the porch.

She smiles up at me. "They don't mind. They're grateful for the work. It's a small job—they'll be done by noon and still have the rest of the day with their families."

I gesture at the bus. "Whose is that contraption?"

Blossom's smile widens into a grin. "That's my humble abode. Depending on her mood, she goes by the Mercy Mobile, the Holy Roller, or—when she won't start—Lucifer's Chariot." She cuts herself off, lips pressed into a line, like the names revealed more than she intended.

My brow shoots up. "You mean you live in that thing?"

Blossom hands out the last coffee and wipes her hands on her apron. "Yes, ma'am. She has all the amenities I need. Mind if I tuck her in your driveway while I'm working on the garden?"

I pause, surprised by the question. Of course it makes sense—practical, even—but something about it feels personal. Permanent. "I guess that's fine. Just don't go planting roots," I say with a forced smile.

She chuckles like I'm joking. I'm not entirely sure I am.

"After I get these fellas started, we can head over to the garden shop. We'll drive Bluebell. She has plenty of room in the rear for our plants."

I narrow my eyes. "How do you know I call her Bluebell?"

Blossom just smiles. "Lucky guess."

"Right." I shake my head, turning away from the railing. "I'm going to grab a bowl of cereal. Let me know when you're ready to go."

As I walk away, I can still feel her smile at my back—warm, knowing, just a little too knowing.

Lucky guess, my foot.

***

I learn more about flowers from Blossom in one morning than I did from my mother in forty-one years.

Blossom is a natural teacher—gentle, encouraging, never making me feel foolish for not knowing the difference between an annual and a perennial.

Flossie, on the other hand, lacked patience and tolerance. She was brilliant, no doubt about that. But if I didn't know something, instead of explaining it to me, she expected me to figure it out on my own. Preferably before I embarrassed her.

By noon, the back of Bluebell is packed with roses, perennials, and several varieties of hydrangeas. I'm determined to get one of every type of hosta—something about their wide, ruffled leaves speaks to me—but Blossom gently steers me toward reason.

"Hostas are shade lovers, Daisy. And you don't have much shade."

We compromise on two sun-tolerant options. "They'll be fine near the fountain," she says, "as long as you keep them watered and mulched."

I'm slowly learning the language of plants and developing a preference for perennials. They're quiet, steady things. They come back year after year without asking much, just a little care and a place to grow.

I gravitate toward flowers with button centers and lacy petals—black-eyed Susans, purple coneflowers, cosmos, zinnias. And of course, daisies. Always daisies.

On the way home, I treat Blossom to lunch at Volta. I order the walnut goat cheese salad with coconut shrimp and Blossom goes for the power bowl with chicken.

An hour later, we arrive back at the house to find the crew gone and the flower beds filled with rich, fresh soil.

Concern creases my brow. "I expected them to still be here. How will I pay them?"

Blossom dismisses me with a flick of her wrist. "Don't worry. They'll send me the bill, and we'll settle up later."

"Okay. If you're sure," I say, lifting the hatch door on the Land Cruiser.

After unloading the plants, we arrange them in the beds to our liking. Once we're satisfied with the layout, we snap plenty of pictures in case anything gets shuffled during planting.

I step back, wiping the sweat from my brow with the back of my hand. The afternoon sun casts long shadows across the flower beds, and for the first time in a long while, the garden feels more full of promise than of loss.

"Let's start digging. Flossie has a collection of shovels for us to choose from," I say, already on my way to the garage.

"But don't you have to prepare for school tomorrow?" Blossom calls after me.

I stop mid-stride, shoulders slumping as I turn back around. "Ugh. I've been procrastinating. But you're right. If I don't start now, I'll be up all night."

"Then you'd better get at it," she says, giving me a gentle nudge toward the house. "I'll work awhile out here, then come up with something for our dinner."

"Dinner?" I ask, patting my belly. "I'm still stuffed from lunch. How can you even think about food?"

Blossom laughs. "I believe in feeding the soul—and it starts with the menu." She taps her chin. "I'm thinking shrimp salad, deviled eggs, and sliced tomatoes."

I lick my lips despite my full stomach. "That does sound good. Thanks, Blossom. You're a godsend."

She lets out a belly laugh. "You have no idea."

I give her a quizzical look, but she's already turning away, heading toward the garage.

I usually work in my bedroom at the small desk Flossie bought me in middle school. But today, I gather my laptop and supplies and head to Dad's study instead. I raise the wooden blinds and open the glass-paned door to the porch. A breeze stirs the honeysuckle, twining around the porch railing —one of the few plants still thriving in the garden. A tune floats in after it. I pause, smiling as Blossom's humming fills the air. "All Things Bright and Beautiful."

I haven't heard that hymn in ages. We used to sing it in church every spring, just as the azaleas started to bloom. Flossie always said it was her favorite—though she never could carry a tune. I remember standing between her and my grandmother in a wooden pew, swaying gently as their voices tangled around mine.

As I settle in at my father's desk chair, the worn leather engulfs me, and the familiar melody warms me like sunlight on skin.

I smile to myself. Blossom is an interesting sort. Wonderful . . . magical . . . unlike anyone I've ever met. It's not just what she says, or the way she hums hymns like she's breathing them. It's something quieter. Something I can't quite name. I want to know more about her—her background, her family—but I sense she'll tell me in time, in her own way.

I open my computer and pull up a file of past syllabi. Two hours pass without a break. I'm so deep in the zone, I don't notice Blossom enter the room until she clears her throat.

"I hate to interrupt," she says softly. "But it's going on seven o'clock. Would you like to eat your dinner in here? I can bring you a tray?"

I glance toward the window, surprised to see the sun dipping low. "I can't believe it's already so late. I got a lot accomplished though. I'm in good shape for tomorrow." I close the computer and push back from the desk.

Blossom wanders the room, her eyes scanning the walls and shelves. "What a cozy spot."

"Too cozy for my liking," I say, standing and stretching. "Although it felt much brighter today with the blinds up and the door open."

"Why don't you paint the walls white?" she muses. "With all these windows, it could feel like a sleeping porch. Add some comfy furniture, a bright rug on the floor, maybe convert the fireplace to gas and tuck in a few birch logs. Line the shelves with your books, and voilà—you've got yourself a perfectly Daisy-like study."

"I'm tempted, but it feels like a crime to cover up wood this beautiful," I say, running my hand across the walnut paneling.

Blossom shoots me a look. "If it's preventing you from enjoying the room, why keep it?"

"Good point." I step back, trying to picture the room washed in white, the windows dressed only in simple woven wooden shades. "I love your ideas. I'll think about it."

I drift over to the built-in bookshelves. "I can't get rid of Dad's books though. He has some rare first editions—many of them signed." I run a finger along the spines until one catches my eye. "Like this one." I pull out a worn copy of *The Sun Also Rises*.

"I knew Ernest," Blossom says casually, like she's talking about a neighbor. "He and I go way back."

My mouth drops open. "How is that even possible? He died in 1961."

Without a word, she pulls out her phone, scrolls for a moment, and turns the screen toward me. A black-and-white photo of Blossom—unmistakably Blossom—standing next to a young, handsome Hemingway on the back of his boat, *Pilar*. He looks about forty, which would date the photo to the late 1930s.

I blink at the screen, then at her. She hasn't aged a day. I shake my head slowly, the question forming before I can stop. "Come clean, Blossom. Who are you? *What* are you? A time traveler or something?"

"Something," Blossom says, leaving me standing there, mouth agape, as she steps onto the porch.

I follow her outside to the railing. "Seriously! You just barged into my life. You're living in a minibus in my driveway, for crying out loud." My voice tightens, sharper than I intend. "I deserve some answers."

"I didn't barge into your life, Daisy," she says, her tone tender. "You invited me in."

A flicker of unease moves through me. "How? When? What do you mean?"

She turns toward me, her gaze steady. "On Saturday night. After you tried to . . ." She hesitates, just for a moment. "You asked God for guidance. For purpose. For a reason to stay."

I lower myself to the bench swing, the events of that night rushing back—the storm, the pills, the pizza deliveryman, the missing pill bottle, the prayer whispered in the dark.

I look up at her, incredulous. "Are you my guardian angel?"

Blossom sits beside me, her voice calm and reassuring. "I prefer to think of myself as a *guiding* angel. I help folks who are standing at a crossroads figure out which path will lead them back to themselves."

I fall back against the bench, pressing my palms to my eyes. "Am I that messed up that I need a guiding angel?"

Blossom gently covers my hand with hers. "You're not messed up, Selwyn. You're human. You've been surviving for so long, you forgot what it feels like to live. That's why I'm here. Not because you're weak—but because you're finally ready to come back to yourself."

A breeze stirs the air between us, and for the first time in a long while, I feel something shifting inside me. Not a fix. But a start.

Six

Keys. Purse. Laptop. I'm halfway down the stairs before I realize I'm missing one of them. Then I remember—I left my laptop in Dad's study. After retrieving it, I head to the kitchen to find Blossom opening and closing cabinet doors like she's hunting for treasure.

"What're you looking for?" I ask, sliding into my sandals.

"Your mama's phone." She taps a finger against the marble countertop. "I'm certain I left it right here last night."

I freeze mid-step. "I remember! We were looking at the photos of her garden." A sick feeling crawls across my skin as my mind flashes back to something else that recently went missing from the kitchen. The pill bottle.

"It must be here somewhere. I wish I could help you look, but I'm already late for class," I say, slinging my work tote over my shoulder.

"Then you need to go. But take your breakfast with you." She hands me a to-go cup of coffee and half an English muffin —covered with orange marmalade. "You can eat in the car on the way. Drive safely."

I smile. "Thank you." I don't ask how she knows I eat an

English muffin with marmalade every morning. Blossom seems to know more about my habits than I do. Having a guiding angel comes with perks.

I arrive in the classroom with only minutes to spare. I much prefer the smaller rooms used for summer school to the cavernous auditoriums where I teach English 101 to hundreds of freshmen.

"Good morning," I say in a cheerful voice.

A few students glance up from their phones with blank faces, but most remain glued to whatever social media post is currently holding their attention.

From the front row, a pretty blonde with bright blue eyes and a pert nose says, "Good morning, Professor Aldridge."

I smile back at her. "Welcome to English 385: Writing the Southern Story."

A wise guy in the back mimics me under his breath. "Welcome to English 385," he says in a singsong voice just loud enough for others to hear.

Here we go, I think. At the start of every term, there's always one—someone who mistakes my calm demeanor, or my age, for weakness.

I drop my tote on the desk with a loud thud. "Let's get one thing straight," I say, my voice calm but firm. "You may think I'm just another professor you can roll your eyes at, but I assure you, I take this course—and your learning—seriously. If that's a problem for you, now's the time to leave. Otherwise, I expect respect, participation, and professionalism from everyone in this room. This class will not be an easy A."

An awkward silence fills the room as the young man shifts in his seat, looking anywhere but at me.

I give him a curt nod. "Glad we understand each other."

Phones disappear—at least for now—as I go over the syllabus, reading list, and expectations. Lately, teaching feels more like endurance than inspiration—but I go through the motions anyway, hoping something sticks.

"That's it for today," I say after about thirty minutes. "Use the next hour to get started on tonight's assignment. We'll meet tomorrow at eight in front of the building for our tour of Faulkner's Life in Oxford. If you're late, you will get left. As we discussed, participation is a key part of your grade."

Chairs scrape, backpacks zip, and the students file out.

Only the pretty blonde remains. "If you have a minute, Professor Aldridge, I need to talk to you about my situation."

"Of course," I say, slipping my laptop into my tote.

She stands, revealing a prominent baby bump. "Would it be possible to turn in assignments early? I'm pressed for time. I may or may not be here for the last week of classes." She places a hand on her belly. "As you can see, I'm very pregnant."

My eyes travel from her face to her baby bump. "Yes, you are."

The color drains from the young woman's face, and she grips the edge of her desk for support.

"Are you okay?" I ask, reaching for her arm.

"I'm not sure. I got dizzy when I stood up. Probably low blood sugar. I didn't eat breakfast."

I guide her gently back into her seat. "You rest for a minute, and I'll be right back. I have some ginger ale and crackers in my office."

I dash down the hall, grab a cold can from the mini fridge, and pull a sleeve of Saltines from the bottom drawer of my desk. When I return to the classroom, she's fanning herself— pale with sweat dotting her brow.

I open the can and place it in her hand. "Here! Drink some of this."

"Thank you." She takes a big gulp, then presses the cold can to her cheek.

"You should probably check in with your doctor?"

She hesitates. "I don't have a doctor. Not an OB anyway. I go to the infirmary whenever I need something. Thankfully, I've been pretty healthy—until now."

I stare at her, trying to process. "You mean you haven't had any testing? No ultrasound? No genetic screening? No diagnostics?"

Her eyes glisten with unshed tears. "I can't afford it."

"What about your parents? The baby's father? Can't they help you?"

She shakes her head slowly. "It's a long story."

I pull up the chair from the desk next to her. "I have time. And you should wait a minute before trying to get back up anyway. What's your name, by the way?"

"Sadie Harper. I'm a double major—creative writing and journalism. I've heard about you. You're kinda legendary among the writing students." She offers a shy smile. "I've tried, but I've never been able to get into any of your classes."

"I'm sorry to hear that," I say, returning her smile. "But I'm glad we'll have this time together. My summer classes tend to be smaller—more personal."

Sadie opens the sleeve of crackers and nibbles the corner of one. "I'm three credits shy of graduating. Fortunately, the university let me walk in May." She pauses. "I didn't tell my parents I was pregnant until they came for graduation. They were furious. They cut me off completely—credit card, allowance, even my car insurance. Good thing I'm paid up for a year. It's only a matter of time before they realize they are still paying for my cell phone." A wry smile tugs at her lips. "They'd already paid for summer school. I've come this far. I can't quit now—not when I'm this close to getting my degree."

"Good for you. Hang in there—only one more class." I glance at her belly. "And the baby's father? Is he a student here?"

"He was. But he left after graduation. No telling where he is now." Sadie shifts in her seat. "We weren't dating. I had a crush on him—stupid, really. We hooked up one night. I was careless, and here we are . . ." She rests a hand on her belly. "He wanted me to get rid of the baby, but I couldn't do that." Her voice hardens. "I made the mistake of telling a few of my sorority sisters that he was the father. Word got out, so now everyone knows. Even so, he refused to take responsibility. Whatever. He's not a good guy. He'd make a lousy father."

"Then we won't give him another thought. What matters now is making sure you and the baby are healthy."

I pull out my phone and thumb off a text.

> Hey, Janey. One of my students needs your help. She's eight months pregnant and has only been seen at the campus infirmary—no testing, no OB. She got dizzy in class this morning. Any chance you can fit her in today?

"What are you doing?" Sadie asks.

"Texting my friend, Janey Sinclair, who is an OB. I'm hoping she can fit you in today."

Sadie straightens, alarm flickering across her face. "But I can't afford a doctor."

"Let me worry about that," I say without hesitation. I'm not sure the Selwyn of a week ago would've offered to help. But I feel strangely connected to this girl. And I have a strong urge to help her. Maybe Blossom is rubbing off on me.

My phone pings with Janey's reply.

> Send her over. I'll let the front desk know she's coming.

I give her text a thumbs up. "Janey wants you to come right over. She's working you in."

Terror fills Sadie's pretty face. "Will you please go with me?"

I pause, surprised by the rawness in her voice. How can I say no when the poor girl has no one?

"Sure," I say, slipping my phone into my bag. "You can ride with me."

I help Sadie to her feet, steadying her before letting go of her arm.

In the parking lot, I open the passenger door of my Land Cruiser.

"Your car is classic, Dr. Aldridge," Sadie says, easing herself inside.

I pull a face, half grinning. "Bluebell and I have been through a lot. You could say we grew up together."

"And you named her! How awesome is that? You're as cool as everyone says."

I can't help but smile as I walk around to the driver's side.

The other students think I'm cool. I thought I was invisible. Maybe—just maybe—I'm not.

Seven

What am I doing on my way to a baby doctor with a pregnant student? I should be home helping Blossom in the garden, elbows deep in mulch—not navigating a prenatal crisis I didn't see coming. But this feels right, somehow. As though I'm meant to be helping her. Now that I have an angel guiding me, maybe I shouldn't question things so much. Maybe I should just go whichever way the wind blows me.

I glance over at Sadie as I exit the campus parking lot. "Where are you living—if you don't mind me asking?"

"In the sorority house." She sighs. "But it's only a matter of time before maintenance discovers me. Then I guess I'll be sleeping in my car."

The image hits hard—a college student, eight months pregnant, curled up in the backseat of some cramped vehicle. Even if it's an SUV, the thought makes my stomach twist. My mind drifts to the three empty bedrooms in my house—quiet, waiting, unused.

I get the impression Sadie hasn't thought this through. Not past summer school. Not past this baby.

"So . . . what about your double major?" I ask. "What do you hope to do?"

Her arms cross over her belly. "Since I was a kid, I've wanted to be an investigative journalist. You know, front lines of history, breaking big stories." She gives a short laugh. "That dream's on hold now. I'll probably end up working in a restaurant or doing copywriting after the baby comes."

I turn into the medical plaza and find a space near the entrance. Shifting the car into park, I say, "I bet if we put our heads together, we can come up with a way for you to earn money and still use that brain of yours."

Sadie turns toward me, her expression brightening for the first time all morning. "Really? I'd love that. Thank you, Professor Aldridge." Her smile fades. "Everyone else has turned their backs on me. It's nice to know someone cares."

I reach for her hand and give it a squeeze. "You're not alone, Sadie. And please—call me Selwyn."

Inside the doctor's office, a young receptionist greets us from behind the desk with a smile. Sadie gives her name, and the receptionist starts typing.

"Can I see your insurance card, please?"

Sadie glances at me, uncertain. "I don't have insurance," she whispers.

I frown. "Your parents never carried a policy for you outside the university's plan?"

A flicker of realization crosses her face. "Oh—wait! Maybe they did. I've never had to use it." She digs into her wallet and pulls out a card. "They might've canceled it by now though."

"Let's find out," the receptionist says, taking the card from her.

Her fingers fly across her keyboard. Then she pauses, her eyes scanning the screen. "Looks like the policy is still active. You're all set." She hands the card back, along with a folder of papers. "There's a lot of helpful information in here, including a QR code that links to our patient portal. Since you're pretty far along, you'll need to complete the hospital preregistration paperwork right away—preferably today."

Sadie takes the packet from her. "Got it."

We've barely settled into our seats when a nurse calls Sadie's name. When I remain seated, Sadie turns to me, her eyes wide with fear. "Please, come with me. I don't want to be alone if there's something wrong with the baby."

"Of course," I say, jumping up. "But think positively. There's nothing wrong with the baby."

The nurse takes Sadie's height and weight, then leads us to an exam room. While Sadie changes into a gown behind the curtain, I pretend to study a chart of a pregnant woman's anatomy, giving her some privacy.

We don't wait long before Janey enters the room. I stand to give her a quick hug. "Thanks for seeing us on such short notice." Gesturing toward Sadie, I add, "This is Sadie Harper —one of my summer school students. She's thirty-six weeks along, and . . . well, there's a lot going on."

Sadie offers a shy smile as she shifts on the table, the paper crinkling beneath her.

"She's been on her own since graduation," I explain. "Her parents cut her off. I'm just trying to help however I can."

Janey's expression softens as she turns to Sadie. "And I will too. We'll take good care of you—I promise."

I step into the hall while Janey performs her exam. A few minutes later, she joins me.

"So far, so good," she says. "Sadie appears to be in excellent health. She's getting dressed now. We'll head down the hall for an ultrasound." Her voice lowers. "What kind of parents abandon their daughter in the middle of a crisis like this?"

I shake my head slowly. "I don't understand it."

A moment later, Sadie emerges, still smoothing her shirt

over her belly. She spots me and smiles. "You're coming with me, right?"

"If that's what you want," I say, and we start down the hall together.

"Do you think I should find out if it's a boy or girl?" she asks, eyes fixed on the floor ahead.

I pause, careful not to influence her. This is her moment—one I never got to experience. "Some people like to plan, others like the mystery. What feels right to you?"

She considers for a beat. "I think I'll wait. I don't have much longer anyway."

"Good choice. There's something magical about waiting until the baby is born," I say, looping my arm through hers as we continue down the hall.

In the dim, quiet ultrasound room, the technician glides the wand over Sadie's belly, and for a few breathless moments, we all watch the monitor. A perfectly formed spine appears, followed by the flicker of a strong, steady heartbeat. Then—ten tiny fingers, ten perfect toes.

Sadie exhales a shaky laugh, her eyes glued to the screen. "Seeing this makes it so real."

The technician steps out, promising to be back in a few minutes with the printouts.

Janey pulls the stool closer to the exam table and rests her hands gently on her knees. "You've done well to make it this far, Sadie, especially on your own. But I want to talk to you woman to woman—off the record."

Sadie nods, wary.

"A baby is a blessing. But it's also a twenty-four-hour job. There's no clocking out. And once that baby is born, every decision you make will matter—for their safety, their health, their future."

Sadie shifts on the table, her hand circling her belly.

"I'm not trying to scare you," Janey continues, "but I need

you to hear this. If, for any reason, Social Services has reason to believe you can't provide adequate care—if the baby shows signs of neglect or if you're living in unsafe conditions—they have the authority to step in. And sometimes, they don't wait."

Sadie's face pales.

"I'm not saying that will happen. I don't want it to happen. But I've seen it. Too many times. And I don't want you to be blindsided."

"What if I . . . I mean, I want this baby. But what if I can't do it all?"

Janey softens, her voice quieting. "Then you build a support system. Start now. Accept help when it's offered. Plan ahead. You're not alone—not if you don't want to be."

Sadie nods, blinking fast.

Janey gives her a moment, then smiles gently. "Okay. Let's get through this next month together, one step at a time."

When Sadie heads to the front desk to schedule her next appointment, I turn to Janey and wrap her in a hug. "Thank you," I whisper in her ear.

She hugs me back. "It was my pleasure. Especially seeing you like this."

I pull away, puzzled. "What do you mean?"

Janey smiles, her eyes soft. "Helping kids in distress suits you, Sel. Maybe more than teaching ever did." She gives my arm a squeeze. "Or maybe you're just a natural-born caregiver."

I start to protest, but nothing comes. The words settle over me—unexpected yet not unwelcome.

Sadie and I ride back to campus in silence, each of us lost in our own thoughts. By the time I pull up in front of her sorority house, I've made my decision. "I'd like for you to come live with me. I have a big house with three empty bedrooms. We can focus on your schoolwork and plan for the baby's arrival."

Sadie blinks, clearly caught off guard. "No! I couldn't impose on you like that. I'll be fine. I have some friends I can stay with."

She says it too quickly, and I suspect she's lying, but I can't force her. "All my contact information is on the syllabus. Call me anytime if you change your mind or need anything."

"I will. And thank you for today. I'm relieved to know the baby's okay."

As I pull away from the curb, I glance in the rearview mirror, half expecting Sadie to wave. She doesn't. She stands on the sidewalk, hugging the folder to her chest, her shoulders squared but her eyes uncertain.

I turn the corner, my hands tightening on the wheel. I imagine her trying to raise a baby while living with her college friends—the ones she just graduated with. The wild parties and late nights . . . not exactly a healthy environment for an infant. But I can't force her into my home, no matter how empty it feels these days. People have to choose their own safe harbors.

The ache that fills me as I drive down Willow Way isn't just worry for Sadie—it's something deeper. For six years, my days were dictated by the needs of others. Medications. Meals. Doctors' appointments. The quiet rhythms of caretaking had become second nature. And now the house echoes in the silence.

Maybe Janey's right. Maybe I am a natural-born caregiver. Or maybe I'm just someone who doesn't know how to be alone.

Eight

When I arrive home just after one, I spot Blossom in the far corner of the garden, kneeling in the dirt with her wide-brimmed hat tilted low to block the midday sun.

"Hey, Blossom!" I call out, waving from the driveway. "I'm sorry I'm late. I got tied up with a student. I'll change and be right out in a minute."

Blossom rises slowly, brushing her hands against her overalls. "Take your time, Daisy. The garden isn't going anywhere. If you're hungry, I left some chicken salad in the refrigerator."

"I'm starving—thank you!" I hadn't realized how hungry I was. I've been too concerned about Sadie to even think about food. But now, the hunger pangs have teeth.

I make my way to the house, but instead of going through the kitchen like always, something pulls me toward Dad's study—as if the room itself is calling me back. It's been lingering in the back of my mind all day. Blossom's suggestion to paint it white, to give it the airy feel of a sleeping porch, is taking root—the idea of soft light and a fresh start. But the moment I step inside, something feels off.

Missing from the second shelf of the bookcase behind his

desk are the framed photos—snapshots of the three of us at birthdays, on vacations, at every milestone. In their place now sits my prize collection of Faulkner novels.

How could this have happened? My Faulkner books were packed neatly in a sealed box under my bed. I pull down the most prized of all—my first edition, signed copy of *As I Lay Dying*. Who on earth would've done such a thing? *Blossom?*

I don't realize I've said her name aloud until I hear her voice from the doorway. "I'm here, Daisy. What's wrong? You're as pale as a ghost."

"We may *have* a ghost, unless you've been snooping around in my bedroom." I wave the book at her. "These books were stored in a box under my bed, and now they're here, where Dad's framed photographs used to be. Did you do this?"

Blossom steps inside, her expression wounded but calm. "No, ma'am. I'd never invade your privacy like that. I've been in the garden most of the day. I came inside now to make sure you got some chicken salad."

"I believe you." Sighing, I sink into Dad's chair and set the book gently on the desk. "Do you believe in ghosts, Blossom? It would explain this—I absently run my hand over the book —and Flossie's missing phone." The missing pill bottle flashes through my mind, but I'm too ashamed of my moment of weakness to say it out loud—not even to my guiding angel.

Blossom lowers herself to the edge of the desk. "Did you seriously just ask an angel if she believes in ghosts?"

I let out an unexpected laugh. "You're an angel, not a ghost. Although, technically, you're both, I guess."

She smiles. "Maybe."

"I was thinking about Flossie anyway—her spirit or soul or whatever you call it. I've heard stories about people getting stuck, not quite making it to the other side. What if she's still here . . . trying to tell me something?"

"That may be," Blossom says, thoughtful. "I usually sense when a spirit is lingering. But I'm not picking up on anything here—not yet anyway."

I drop my gaze, my eyes landing on a sheet of paper resting near the edge of the desk. "What's this?" I murmur, picking it up. It's a drawing—an ink sketch of a pregnant young woman, her head bowed, one hand resting on her rounded belly. The resemblance to Sadie is unsettling.

"Okay, now I'm really freaked out." I hand the drawing to Blossom. "This is Sadie, the student I was tied up with today."

Blossom tilts her head one way and another. "A pregnant student. Now that's a story I'd like to hear. Shall we move to the kitchen? You need to eat lunch, and I could use a spot of Rosa's sun tea."

I rocket out of the chair. "Rosa! I should've warned you. Did you meet her today? You didn't tell her you're a . . . you know . . . about your background, did you?"

Blossom lifts a calming hand. "Rosa and I met. She's perfectly lovely. And no, I only share my *background* to my soul seekers."

I tilt my head. "Your who?"

A twinkle lights her eyes. "My soul seekers. People like you —searching for something, even if they don't quite know what it is yet." She hands me back the drawing. "Rosa mentioned a doctor's appointment this afternoon. I believe she told you?"

I nod, sheepish. "She did, but I forgot. I'm glad you two met. Rosa has been with my family since I was a little girl."

Blossom smiles genuinely. "And she thinks highly of you. Like you're her own."

Her words catch me off guard. I study her, wondering what exactly they talked about while I was out.

"We had an interesting discussion in Spanish. She's still

quite lingual, you know? It's such a shame she hasn't been to Mexico to visit her family in over ten years."

Guilt rises in my chest. "After all she's done for my family, I should send her on that trip," I murmur, already halfway to the kitchen.

I go through the motions—scooping chicken salad onto a plate, adding a spoonful of fresh fruit from the container Rosa always keeps stocked—but I can't stop thinking about the drawing. I sit down and stir the chicken salad with my fork, appetite gone. The sketch lies beside me on the counter like a taunt.

"This is really bugging me, Blossom," I say, eyes locked on the paper. "Whoever did this had to be following me today. How else would they know about Sadie?" I glance up. "Have you seen any strangers lurking around? Anyone who doesn't belong?"

Blossom doesn't answer right away. She picks up the drawing again, her brow furrowed, then sets her steady gaze on me. "This doesn't feel like the work of a stranger. Whoever's doing these things—taking your mama's phone, rearranging your possessions . . . I don't think they're doing it to scare you, Daisy. They're trying to be seen. Or maybe . . . remembered." She sets the drawing down with care, as if it's more than paper and ink.

I knit my brow. "If they're trying to be seen, then why not just show themselves?"

Blossom shrugs. "Maybe they're afraid. He—or she— might need a little more time." She sits down on the stool next to me, her hands wrapped around her tea glass. "Now. Tell me about Sadie."

I smile, the tension in my shoulders easing a little. "She's a sweet girl—a pretty little blonde. Never been in my classes before, but she seemed genuinely engaged. Which is rare these days."

I tell her about Sadie—how she got dizzy in class, how she hasn't had proper medical care until now. I explain that I took her to see Janey and offered to let her stay here.

When I look over at Blossom, she's grinning at me like she knows something I don't.

"What?" I ask.

"Oh, nothing," she says, far too innocently.

I jab her with my elbow. "Tell me."

She chuckles. "You've found someone new to care about. You're a natural-born caregiver, Daisy."

A natural-born caregiver? That's what Janey called me.

"I'm not a natural-born anything, Blossom." I glance down at my plate, pushing a grape around with my fork. "But someone needs to help this girl. Her parents cut her off, and she's camping out in the sorority house. It's only a matter of time before she gets kicked out."

Pushing my plate away, I pick up my phone and start searching for a number.

"What're you doing?" Blossom asks, brow furrowed.

"Calling my mother's painting contractor. I need to de-Flossie this house."

Blossom scrunches her face in confusion. "De-Flossie?"

"If Sadie ends up staying here, I don't want to subject her to this technicolor madness," I say, gesturing at the walls—even though the chartreuse and white geometric lattice pattern is the only wallpaper in the house I actually like. "Sadie says she has friends she can stay with, but let's be real—kids vanish from Oxford faster than beer at a tailgate after graduation."

Clicking on the contact information for Old Town Finishes, I introduce myself and tell the receptionist why I'm calling. She transfers me, and Buck Tisdale picks up right away.

"I was so sorry to hear about Flossie. Your mama was a mess—and I mean that fondly. I dearly loved that woman.

Painting that house was like stepping inside a box of crayons. Took me three days just to find a white wall."

I laugh. "Wait! I'm pretty sure there *are* no white walls in this house."

He laughs with me.

"Which is exactly why I want to tone things down—soon. I'm having a guest come for an extended stay, and I'd like to paint the entire interior."

Buck hesitates. "Would tomorrow be too soon? I had a client cancel at the last minute—she's having a full-blown crisis over color choices, if you can believe it. Been on the waiting list for six months. I've got two crews lined up and nowhere to send them."

I glance at Blossom, who nods encouragingly. "I can make tomorrow work."

"Excellent. Are you at home now? I can swing by, take a look, and give you an estimate. We can talk colors while I'm there."

"I'm here. I'll see you in a few."

I end the call and set the phone on the counter. "Why would anyone cancel at the last minute after waiting six months to have their house painted? Choosing paint colors can't be *that* hard, can it?" I look up at Blossom, who is grinning like the cat who swallowed the canary. "What'd you do?"

She drags an imaginary zipper across her lips.

"You arranged that last-minute cancellation, didn't you?"

"I'll never tell," she says, rolling her eyes toward the ceiling.

"Well, I won't be looking that gift horse in the mouth. And I'm certainly not having a color crisis. I'm painting the entire house the same shade of off-white or light taupe— except Dad's study, which will be all white, per your suggestion." I glance around. "Only this room gets a pass. The wallpaper's relatively new. Flossie renovated the kitchen right before Dad got sick. And I actually like this pattern."

Blossom smiles. "I like it too. It feels fresh." She gets up and places her empty glass in the dishwasher. "You'd be surprised at how many choices there are for off-white and light taupe. After the contractor leaves, we'll pay a visit to the paint store, and I'll point out a few of my favorites."

I smirk. "Lord, help me if I start naming paint colors."

Outside, a truck rumbles up the drive. I hear the familiar clang of a metal ladder. Buck Tisdale has arrived. And ready or not, Flossie's house is about to change. I just hope she doesn't haunt me for it—if she's not the one already haunting me.

Nine

Blossom and I lose track of time at the Benjamin Moore store, poring over swatches like we're solving a mystery. We narrow our options from more than fifty to three—Edgecomb Gray, Classic Gray, and Balboa Mist. Trusting Blossom's eye, I go with Balboa Mist. It carries a quiet sophistication—less cozy farmhouse, more understated elegance. A touch formal, but never cold. It pairs beautifully with Chantilly Lace, the bright white trim Flossie fell in love with during her last renovation.

The shift from Flossie's high-drama palette to something softer feels like more than a design choice. It's a passing of the torch—from mother to daughter—quiet, but final. A whisper of calm where there was once a shout. And yet, as I hold the paint swatch in my hand, I wonder if I'm softening the house, or erasing her? Is this who I've always been . . . or who I've become without her?

We step out into the sunlight, the scent of paint still clinging to my clothes. I unlock the car, juggling a handful of swatches.

Without thinking, I murmur, "I wonder if I'll ever be the kind of woman my mother was."

Blossom pauses, one hand on the passenger door. "You won't."

"I'm sorry?" I ask, even though the words are still echoing in my mind.

She smiles, but her emerald eyes are intense. "Your mother lived loud, Daisy. She filled every room—sometimes with laughter, sometimes with heat. But you . . . you fill a space differently. Softer. Quieter. That doesn't make you less. Just makes you *you*."

I open the car door, her words pressing into me like sunlight through glass—warming, but impossible to hold.

I start the engine, pausing before putting the car in gear. "So, you think it's okay for me to change the house? You don't think Flossie would mind?"

Blossom doesn't answer right away. She rests her hand lightly on my arm, grounding me. "She might mind," she says, her voice gentle but sure. "But that's not the question."

I turn to look at her, unprepared for the clarity in her green eyes. "What's the question?"

"Are you living in her house—or yours?"

Her honesty stings a little—but it's the kind of sting that wakes you up. It's a relief of sorts. No sugarcoating. No walking on eggshells. Just the plain truth.

I shift the car into reverse. "Mine," I say, more to myself than to her.

And for the first time in a long while, I believe it.

Excitement flutters across my chest as I imagine *my* furniture—pieces that have never lived in this house—replacing Flossie's. Clean lines, soft tones, rooms washed in Balboa Mist. A space that feels like me.

I pull into the driveway, but I don't turn off the engine. "I'm going to run over to my storage unit. I haven't seen my furniture in six years, and I need to reacquaint myself with my things." An unexpected warmth floods me. "When I was first out on my own, I saved for months to buy a faux bamboo bed —Spanish cedar, beautifully made. I was so proud of it." I glance at Blossom and smile. "Suddenly, I can't wait to see it again."

"Sounds lovely. I imagine you'll find more than a few things you've forgotten." She opens her car door. "After dinner, we'll pack up the contents of your bookshelves and anything else you don't want the painters handling."

"Ugh. I didn't think about that, but you're right. We'll need some boxes too."

"I'll work on that while you're gone," Blossom says. "See you soon."

On the drive across town to the storage facility, I picture my bed in what used to be my parents' room—paired with Flossie's handsome mahogany tall chest, robin's egg blue lamps, and creamy wool carpet.

I'll replace her heavy curtains with plantation shutters. Let the light in. Let the room breathe. The more I think about it, the more I like the idea of installing shutters in all the rooms.

At the gate, I punch in my security code, the keypad blinking to life with a slow green light. I drive through, winding past row after row of identical units. It's been so long, I can't remember which one is mine. After circling twice— maybe three times—I finally find it. My heart skips as the key turns in the lock. I slide the door up and stare at my things, crammed into the too-small space.

I was still raw from my divorce when the movers brought everything over from the house I'd once shared with my husband. Numb and exhausted, I barely paid any attention when they packed everything in—whichever way it would fit.

I wedge my body through the narrow aisle they left me, inching my way to the back. The largest piece of my sectional sofa leans on end against the left wall. On the right, I spot my black-lacquered Chinese mirror, covered in dust, the carved frame just visible beneath the grime. The sight of my creamy sleigh crib takes my breath away, leaving an old hollow ache in my chest—one I haven't felt in years. I'd been premature, decorating a nursery before there was even a baby to fill it. Maybe that was the problem. Maybe I jinxed myself, daring to believe too soon.

If Sadie moves in with me, her baby will use it. At least for a little while.

Finally, I reach the back of the unit. I'm running my hand along the warm, golden Spanish cedar of my bed's headboard when, all at once, something behind me shifts. I spin around, heart pounding, just in time to see my wing chair topple forward and land squarely in the narrow aisle behind me, blocking my path. I try to shove it out of the way, but it's wedged tight between a mahogany chest and my Queen Anne desk. No give. No wiggle room. No way out.

Don't panic. Don't panic. Don't panic.

Someone in the office will rescue me. I'll get the contact information online. I tug my phone out of my pocket, but there's no cell service inside the corrugated metal unit. I step onto a small square side table. Still no bars. Desperate, I climb onto a chest of drawers, waving my phone above my head. Nothing.

Fear prickles at the edges now. I scramble back down to the floor, heart hammering, sweat trickling down my back. The furniture looms around me, boxing me in.

When I came in, I'd been too busy searching for my unit to notice if anyone else was around.

"Hello! Is anyone out there? Can you help me? I'm stuck in here," I call out again and again until my throat is dry.

Finally—"Selwyn? Is that you?"

Not just anyone. Someone who knows me. His voice is faint but familiar. *Griffin.*

"Yes! I'm in the back. The armchair fell, and it's blocking my path."

"Hold on. I'm coming."

I hear rustling on the other side of the wall of furniture as he makes his way toward me. There's a yelp, followed by a muttered curse.

"Are you all right?" I call out. He can't help me out if he gets stuck too.

"Yeah, just banged my knee. Almost there."

There's more groaning as he wrestles the chair out of the way. Then suddenly the path is clear, and there stands Griffin.

Relief crashes over me, and on impulse, I throw myself into his arms. "Thank you! I was beginning to worry I might have to spend the night in here."

The feel of him—solid and familiar—is both comforting and unsettling, stirring up memories I'm not ready to revisit.

"I'm glad I came along when I did." He takes my hand. "Let's get you out of here."

Griffin guides me back through the narrow tunnel toward the front, careful to keep me close. "Your furniture is really stuffed in here," he says, half laughing. "Was this your doing?"

"The movers," I say, lowering the rolling door and snapping the padlock back in place. "After my divorce."

Griffin wanders over to my Land Cruiser, running a hand along the front fender. "I see you're still driving old Bluebell. How many miles do you have on her now?"

"Close to eight hundred thousand," I say, brushing dust from my jeans. "I've rebuilt the engine twice."

He lets out a low whistle. "That's incredible."

"Everyone thinks I'm crazy for not buying a new car. At least a newer version of Bluebell. But I can't give her up."

An awkward silence settles over us. Griffin kicks at a pebble on the pavement, sending it skittering. "I'm glad I ran into you," he says, finally. "I've been wanting to apologize for the other day. It was insensitive of me to ask about selling your house so soon after Flossie's death. I just moved back to town, and I'm desperate for a listing."

"I forgive you. We're even since you just saved me from furniture prison." I turn to open my car door, then glance back at him, my voice quieter. "But that doesn't mean we're friends. I'll never forgive you for breaking my heart."

Shame burns my cheeks as I speed out of the parking lot. After more than twenty years, I thought I was over the hurt of his betrayal.

I say as much to Blossom when I find her grilling salmon steaks on the back porch. "What is wrong with me that I can't get over a high school romance?"

Blossom smiles softly as she flips a steak. "No one ever really gets over their first love, Daisy. Some people are woven into you, thread by thread. Pulling them out would mean unraveling who you are. But you get better at pretending it was just a phase . . . until you run into him at a storage unit and remember exactly how it felt."

"Yeah. I guess you're right." I peer over her shoulder at the salmon steaks. "Those look delicious."

"Should be done soon. After we eat, we can get started on the packing. We don't want to hold the painters up in the morning."

"For sure." With two crews, Buck Tisdale promised to be done by Friday, which will give me the weekend to swap out furniture from my storage unit.

Entering the kitchen, I grab a glass and fill it with water at the sink. Out of the corner of my eyes, I spot something on the counter. A paint swatch—the Balboa Mist I chose—and another drawing. My stomach drops as I step closer. It's a sketch of Griffin and me, standing beside Bluebell, caught in mid-conversation.

Blossom's words echo in my mind. *This doesn't feel like the work of a stranger. I don't think they're doing it to scare you, Daisy. They're trying to be seen. Or maybe . . . remembered.* But by who? Someone I know? Someone from my past? Or someone I haven't met yet?"

The back door swings open, and Blossom breezes in, carrying the plate of salmon steaks. "What's wrong, Daisy? You're white as a sheet."

I hand her the drawing and paint chip. "Did you see anyone coming or going from the house?"

She shakes her head, studying the sketch. "Nope. I've been in the kitchen since you dropped me off. Except when I stepped outside to grill. Must've slipped in through the front door when I wasn't looking." Blossom chuckles, unbothered. "I'm intrigued. It feels harmless to me, not vindictive, not threatening. She . . . or he . . . is trying to get your attention. I think it's kinda sweet."

"Well, I think it's kinda creepy, always watching me. The *Watcher.* What makes you think they're trying to get my attention?"

"Just a hunch." She rests a reassuring hand on my shoulder. "I won't let anything happen to you, Daisy. That much I can promise." She squeezes. "But we should stay on high alert. The sooner we find the little rascal, the better."

Ten

I've only known Blossom a few days, but so far, her hunches have been spot-on. So, when she casually mentions that Sadie might move in soon, my hopes do what they always do—rise too fast, too high.

"I wouldn't count on it," I say more to myself than to Blossom. "She might still find a friend to live with."

"Maybe. But just in case, we should pack the upstairs first. We'll have the painters start up here tomorrow. That way, if she decides to come, we'll have a room ready for her."

"Good idea," I say, traipsing up the stairs behind her with two empty boxes balanced in my arms.

We leave our boxes at the top of the stairs while I give Blossom a quick tour of the second floor.

I show her my room first—the sunny corner bedroom overlooking the street. "Sadie can take this one. It's quiet and there's plenty of light. She can use my desk for her schoolwork."

We cross the hall to the opposite corner. This room is nearly bare, save for a daybed pushed against the wall. "This will be the nursery," I say, pausing in the doorway. "Flossie used to call it her craft room, but I never once saw her thread a needle—much less sew on a button."

Next up is the guest room—featuring a queen bed, pristine linens, and a faint scent of lavender sachets. I was never allowed in here. This room was strictly reserved for guests we never had. Flossie kept it spotless, just in case someone from out of town might suddenly appear and need a place to stay. But the truth is, everyone we knew lived in Oxford. No one ever came.

I run my hand along the smooth bedspread, untouched by time. "It's funny, isn't it? All this fuss over a room no one ever used."

Blossom peers around, nodding thoughtfully. "Sometimes people keep rooms like this not for who might come but for who never did."

Her words land softly. "Exactly. That's classic Flossie—always ready, always polished, even if no one ever came. That room wasn't just for guests. It was a monument to what she hoped for. A kind of shrine to connection, to possibility . . . to people who never showed up."

We carry our boxes down the hall to my parents' room, a spacious retreat that stretches the width of the house with sweeping views of the backyard. I pause in the doorway, taking it all in. "I'm not sure I can sleep in here." Flossie cleared out most of my father's things after he died, but her dresser is still cluttered with her perfume bottles. "Will it ever stop feeling like theirs?"

"Of course," Blossom says, circling the room. "As soon as the walls are painted and your bed's in place." She pauses, taking it in. "It would be a shame to let such a lovely room sit unoccupied."

"True. Just like Dad's study," I say, disappearing into Flossie's closet with my boxes.

I spend an hour going through her extensive wardrobe of

designer labels. I save two pieces, both as outlandish as they are unforgettable. The first is a short, fun fur jacket, snowy white with streaks of blush pink woven through, like someone had taken a paintbrush to fresh snow. It still smells faintly of her—Chanel No. 5 and a hint of hairspray. The second is a silk caftan, all swirling jewel tones and gold embroidery, the kind of dress she wore to cocktail parties when she wanted to make an entrance. Neither piece fits my style—or my life—but somehow, parting with them feels impossible.

I'm grateful Flossie wasn't a hoarder. She routinely purged closets, having a major clean-out every few years.

After packing the few accessories in the guest room, I move on to mine, which takes another hour. But as I work, I feel a flicker of excitement about the prospect of moving into the master suite once the painting is complete.

By the time I get downstairs, Blossom has already made major headway with the bookcases, both in the living room and Dad's study.

"Aren't you glad I opted not to paint the kitchen?" I say to Blossom when we finish around midnight. "We'd be up all night emptying these cabinets."

She chuckles. "These cabinets are new. They don't need painting. And I'd hate to see you get rid of this cheerful wallpaper. It puts me in a good mood every morning when I'm putzing around in here."

I smile. "It does, doesn't it?"

As we drag ourselves toward bed, I glance once more at the kitchen and remember all the quiet mornings I spent here with Flossie, sipping coffee while her memories slowly slipped away. Funny how the room still feels full of her, even now.

I'm disappointed—and a little concerned—when Sadie doesn't make roll call for our Faulkner tour of Oxford on Wednesday morning. Despite having warned them yesterday that I wouldn't wait, I give the handful of stragglers a few extra minutes. But Sadie isn't among them, and I have no choice but to head out on the tour.

Twenty minutes later, we're gathered in front of Rowan Oak—William Faulkner's beautiful Greek Revival home, where he lived and wrote for more than thirty years—when Sadie quietly joins our group. She doesn't say much—just hovers on the edges—but listens intently and takes notes diligently as I begin my lecture about Faulkner's complicated life and legacy.

I'm pleased to see a few other students are equally engaged, and when the tour ends in front of Bondurant Hall later that morning, the whole group begs for more field trips.

"I applaud your enthusiasm," I say with a chuckle. "Don't worry. There will be others. And don't forget—your first assignment is due tomorrow. After today's tour and our introduction into Faulkner's life, I can't wait to hear your thoughts on *place*—what it means to you, how it shapes identity, and how it might shape a story."

The others scurry off in a tangle of backpacks and flip-flops. But Sadie lingers behind. "I'm sorry I was late for the tour, Professor Aldridge."

I give her a look, and she corrects herself. "I mean, Selwyn." Her voice wavers. "I got kicked out of the sorority house this morning." Tears well in her eyes. "The woman from housing was awful. She wouldn't even give me until this afternoon to move out."

My chest tightens. "Did you have to move everything out yourself? In your condition?"

Sadie nods, eyes lowered. "Down three flights of stairs to my car."

"That's inexcusable. I'm so sorry. You should've called me —I would've helped." I hesitate, then add gently, "Did you find a place to stay? If not, my offer still stands."

She swipes at her eyes. "All my friends have left town. But I wouldn't want to impose on you. I need a place until after the baby comes—until I can figure things out. But that's asking too much."

I rest a hand on her shoulder. "I offered, Sadie. I have plenty of room, and honestly, I would enjoy the company."

Uncertainty crosses her face, a flicker of hesitation I can't read.

"Why don't we drive over there now?" I suggest. "I can show you the house, and then you can decide. No pressure either way. It's your decision. I promise."

Sadie slowly nods. "I guess that would be okay," she says, the kind of yes that comes from someone who's learned not to trust too easily.

My heart aches for her—for the way she braces herself against disappointment, even when kindness is all that's being offered.

"Great. Let me just run inside and get my things. I'll meet you in the parking lot. You can't miss my car."

This brings a smile to her face. "I love Bluebell."

I grab my belongings, lock my office, and head back outside. When I reach my car, Sadie is leaning against the front passenger side, twirling a strand of blonde hair while staring at her phone—like she's willing it to ring.

On the drive through town, I explain about moving home after the divorce to help my mother care for my sick father. "Then Flossie got sick with early-onset Alzheimer's, and I stayed three more years. Now they're both gone, and I'm alone in the house."

Sadie crinkles her nose. "You called your mama Flossie?"

I laugh. "Yes! Everyone did—even my friends when we

were kids. She was one of a kind." I pause, my voice softening. "She died last week."

"Oh, no! I'm so sorry." Sadie squirms uncomfortably in her seat. "Seriously, Selwyn—if it's too much for me to stay with you . . ." Her voice trails off.

"Not at all." I shake my head. "The house is empty without Flossie. You would be doing me a favor." I pause, then add, "But there's something you should know."

Sadie tenses, clearly bracing for the worst. "What is it?"

"I'm having the interior painted. They say it'll be finished by Friday, but it might be a bit of a mess until then."

"I don't mind," she says quickly. "My mother's an interior designer. She's always redecorating." She scrunches up her face, as if a thought just occurred to her. "You don't think the paint fumes will hurt the baby, do you?"

"I don't think so, but we'll ask Janey just to be sure." I smile over at her, hoping to ease the worry creasing her brow. "I'm planning to swap out some of Flossie's furnishings for my own. You can help me decide what goes where. I even have a crib in storage."

Her face lights up. "I didn't realize you have a kid."

My smile fades. "I don't. It wasn't in the cards for me. But I had high hopes once. Hence the crib."

We arrive at home to find paint trucks lining the curb in front of the house, and Rosa and Blossom carrying on like old childhood friends in the kitchen, laughing over something as though they've known each other for years.

Sadie leans in close to me. "You have two housekeepers?" she asks, her blue eyes wide.

I laugh. "No, Rosa's been with our family since I was a little girl. Blossom's just helping me bring Flossie's backyard garden back to life."

I turn toward the women and gesture for Sadie to step forward. "Everyone, this is my friend—and student—Sadie.

I'm hoping to convince her to stay with me until the baby comes."

Rosa clasps her hands over her heart, her expression tender. "Oh, I hope you do, querida. A baby is just what this house needs. What we all need."

Blossom sets down the dishtowel she's holding. "Ain't that the truth," she says, winking at Sadie. "You'd be the best thing to happen to Willow Way since porch swings and sweet tea on summer nights."

Sadie lays a hand over her belly, her eyes glistening. "Y'all are too kind," she murmurs, voice thick with emotion.

Blossom's smile deepens. "We're just telling the truth, sugar. Sometimes life gives you a soft place to land—just when you need it most."

I nudge Sadie gently toward the hallway. "Come on. I'll show you the upstairs."

We weave our way around ladders and paint cans to the stairs. The mob of painters has finished the upstairs and are making their way down.

Sadie pauses to study the color, tilting her head one way and another. "This is Balboa Mist, isn't it?"

I stop on the stair above her. "You have a good eye!"

She offers a sad smile. "It's one of my mother's favorite paint colors. It's a perfect choice for a whole house—especially one as graceful as this."

"Blossom gets the credit. But I'm pleased with the choice," I say, continuing up the stairs ahead of her.

I lead her into my old bedroom. The transformation is lovely—the sunny yellow walls replaced by the serene taupe. "You'll stay here, in my old room. There's plenty of space for your things, and you can use my desk for your classwork. We'll set up the nursery right across the hall."

Sadie looks around, wide-eyed. "This is lovely. But where will you sleep?"

"I'm moving into the master suite," I explain. "You'll have the hall bathroom all to yourself."

"And it'll be just the two of us living here?" The first spark of real hope lights up her face.

I nod. "And the baby, once he or she arrives."

"But I can't pay you, Selwyn. I have no money. I can't even put gas in my car," Sadie says, her voice trembling.

I pull her into a hug. "You don't deserve to have everyone turn their backs on you, Sadie. You made a mistake—you got pregnant. So what? Worse things have happened." I pull back just enough to meet her eyes. "I'm offering because I want to help. And selfishly? You'd be doing me a favor. This house feels too big, too quiet without Flossie. Helping you get ready for the baby might be just the kind of purpose I need right now."

Sadie's eyes are glassy, but there's the faintest hint of a smile. "I guess we really need each other right now," she says, her voice barely above a whisper.

I grin. "Is that a yes?"

She nods. "I think so."

"Yay! I'm thrilled." I drop my arms from around her. "We're going to have so much fun getting ready for this baby. But first we need to air out this room." As I throw open a window, I smile to myself, remembering the bird I let in the house the last time I left all the windows open. Fortunately, the upstairs windows have screens.

"I'll text Janey—just to be sure about the paint fumes," I add, pulling out my phone.

We leave the room, retracing our steps back down the stairs.

"Are you ready for me to drive you back to campus for your car?" I ask.

Sadie moves toward the front door. "If you don't mind, I think I'll walk. I could use a little fresh air."

"Of course. It's only a few blocks." I open the door, and we step onto the front porch. "I'll be out in the garden with Blossom when you get back. We can help you unload your things, then you can set up at the kitchen table to work on your paper. It might be a little noisy with the painters."

Sadie smiles—a real one this time. "I don't mind. I have noise-canceling earbuds."

Then, surprising me, she leans in and presses her cheek against mine. "Thank you, Selwyn. For everything." She pulls back, her eyes shining. "You're a really good person."

Before I can respond, she steps down onto the sidewalk, one hand resting protectively on her belly.

I watch her go, part of me wanting to call her back, but the bigger part knowing she needs this—a moment to breathe. Space to reclaim something she thought she'd lost—control.

Eleven

Blossom puts me in charge of a modest corner of the garden, the one reserved for annuals. It feels like a small vote of confidence. She shows me how to dig the holes, carefully remove the plants from the plastic containers, and gently loosen their tender roots before placing them in the ground. "Tuck the soil back in gently—like you're tucking a baby into bed."

The scent of fresh earth rises around me as I work, and a quiet peace settles over me—the simple, steady rhythm of digging, planting, tucking each new life gently into place.

"What do you think of Sadie?" I ask Blossom as I sink my shovel into the ground.

Sadie had returned from campus and was now diligently working away on her paper at the kitchen table. Upstairs, Rosa was giving the bedrooms a thorough cleaning. Once the painters finished this afternoon, we'd help Sadie carry her things upstairs and settle into our respective bedrooms.

Blossom leans on her shovel, smiling faintly. "She seems nice enough. It's you I'm worried about?"

I look up, frowning. "Me? How so?"

"I'm worried you'll get too attached to the young mama

and her baby when it comes. You've experienced enough loss these past few years. I'd hate to see you hurt again."

I lower my gaze, focusing on the hole I'm digging. "I'll live. I've survived the loss of two parents. I'll survive this too." I press the shovel deeper into the soil. "Besides, Sadie has no one else. Someone has to help her. When the time is right, I want her to move on from Oxford—to find her way in the world."

"That's the best kind of help, Daisy. The kind that lifts someone up without clipping their wings. You're giving her what she needs, not what makes *you* feel better." Blossom smiles down at me. "I'm glad you're thinking ahead. Who knows? You might find another troubled student to help. Maybe this is a new path for your future."

I choke out a laugh. "Are you suggesting I operate a halfway house for wayward students?"

Blossom grins. "Maybe. Stranger things have happened." Her gaze drifts past me, and her smile shifts into something softer. "Speaking of your future . . . there's a handsome young man here to see you."

I turn, following her gaze. Griffin is walking toward me, his loping gait easily recognizable. A smile tugs at my mouth—automatic, unguarded. But even as my heart stirs, I shake my head and murmur, "That's not my future. That's my past."

I stand slowly, wiping my forehead with the back of my gloved hand. "Griffin. What're you doing here?"

"I was in the neighborhood and thought I'd stop by." He nods politely at Blossom. "Afternoon, ma'am. I'm Griffin McRae."

Blossom flashes him a bright smile. "Nice to meet you, Griffin. My friends call me Blossom. I'm helping Selwyn restore her mama's garden."

Griffin glances around, his expression softening. "Miss Flossie sure loved her garden." His lips part in a reminiscent smile. "She caught me picking flowers for Selwyn once. I thought she was going to tan my behind."

I laugh out loud at the memory. "I remember! She was hopping mad at you."

He looks back at me, his face now serious. "Can you spare a minute? I need to talk to you about something."

"Sure. Let's go up to the porch."

I must look a mess, I think as I lead him up to the house. My hair is pulled back in a stubby ponytail. I'm dressed in cutoffs and a worn Ole Miss T-shirt. I probably have dirt smeared all over my face.

"Do you want something to drink?" I ask as we reach the porch.

"I'm fine, but thanks."

We sit down together on the bench swing, and the memories flood in—uninvited, vivid. Summer nights spent holding hands. Waiting until my parents went to bed to turn out the porch light. Making out under the stars, the moon shining in the distance. My heart pounding as I waited for him to pick me up for a date. And later—sitting right here with tears streaming down my face—that frigid night he broke my heart. Funny how the same swing could hold so much joy and so much sorrow—and still feel like home.

"Selwyn," Griffin says, his voice softer now, almost hesitant. "I never meant to hurt you. I don't think I even realized, back then, how much I did."

I blink, pulled out of that cold night of memory and into the sunlight of this one.

Griffin leans forward, elbows on his knees, staring down at his hands. "I was young. Selfish. Caught up in what I thought I wanted." He shakes his head, a sad, almost embarrassed smile tugging at his mouth. "Eleanor seemed perfect. Poised. Prominent. The kind of person I thought I wanted. How wrong I was about her. She nearly destroyed my life." He finally looks up, and the regret in his eyes almost undoes me.

"She *destroyed* your life?" I ask, my voice cool. "That's a pretty strong statement, Griffin."

He nods, slow and grim. "But it's true. Eleanor is greedy and shallow. I could never give her enough. I went bankrupt trying to support her in the lifestyle she thought she deserved."

I stare at him. "Seriously, Griffin? Bankrupt." I'm about to accuse him of exaggerating when I see the hollow look in his eyes.

"It's true," he says, his voice flat. "She was desperate to join a country club. It's all she ever talked about. I let her cloud my judgement, made a bad real estate investment, and lost everything." He scrubs a hand over his face, like he's trying to wipe the memory away. "Eleanor left me, took our two young daughters, and told the court I was abusive. The judge gave her full custody." His voice roughens. "She's turning them into mini versions of herself."

I let go of the swing's chain, not even realizing I'd been clinging to it. I'd been holding onto my anger—the hurt, the betrayal—for more than twenty years. But now, watching him —shoulders slumped, pride stripped away—I just feel sad. Sad for the boy he was. Sad for the man he became. Sad for everything we might have been, if we'd only known better.

"Thanks for telling me, Griff. I'm sorry for all you've been through."

He rests an arm along the back of the swing, and for a moment, the years between us seem to fall away.

"Believe it or not, Selwyn, I've thought a lot about you over the years—what our lives would've been like if I'd made different choices. If I'd realized how lucky I was to have you." He shifts uncomfortably, glancing away before meeting my eyes again. "Yesterday, at the storage unit, you said we're not friends. I realize it's asking a lot, but I wish you'd reconsider.

All my old friends have moved on without me. They have full lives with wives and children. They don't have time for me, a lonely soon-to-be divorcé."

His words soften something deep inside me. It's impossible not to feel his pain. But even as my heart aches for the boy he was—and the man he's become—I know better now. I'm not the girl who would lose herself trying to fix him anymore.

"Believe it or not, it's the same for me," I say, offering a small smile to lighten the mood. "And I never even moved away."

His head tilts, curiosity flickering across his face. "Really? How?"

"My friends started having children, and I couldn't. We traveled different paths—further and further apart."

Understanding crosses his face. "I can see how that might happen. Funny how the lives you dream of having at seventeen can slip away while you're busy surviving."

"I guess we both learned that the hard way."

He gives me a silly grin that I remember all too well. "So . . . about that friendship . . . Can we try again?"

"As long as friendship is all you're offering. Because I can't go down that road with you again, Griff."

He holds up three fingers. "That's all I want. Scout's honor."

I nod curtly. "Okay. Friendship it is. I have an extra shovel if you'd like to help us plant."

He chuckles as he stands. "I would love to help, but I need to get back to work. I'm showing a house in an hour."

We walk down the porch steps together toward his Tahoe.

"I noticed the painting contractor's trucks out front," he says, glancing back at the house. "I'm asking as a friend, not a real estate agent. Are you putting it on the market?"

"On the contrary. I'm transitioning it from Flossie's technicolor wonderland to something a little more livable. That's why I was at my storage facility yesterday. Looking to see what I might want to bring over here."

"Good for you. I know a couple of young guys who have started a moving company—Cash and Colby Harlan, twin brothers. They'd appreciate the business."

Jack Brunson—the *Jack of Trades* from the medical supply company—comes to mind. He'd offered to haul off Flossie's mildewed sofa in his truck, but I have a hunch this job is too big for him.

"Cool. I'd love to talk to them. I haven't figured out how to go about making the move. I want to switch out some of Flossie's things for mine."

"Cash and Colby will know how to handle it. The name of their company is Muscle and Hustle." He pulls out his phone. "Give me your number, and I'll text you their contact information."

I call out my number as he thumbs it into his phone.

"Be sure to tell them I sent you," he says, tossing his phone onto the console, then climbing into the Tahoe after it.

As I watch him drive away, Blossom—who has somehow snuck up behind me—clears her throat near my ear. I jump. "Geez, Blossom. Don't sneak up on me like that."

She chuckles, unbothered. "He seems like a nice young man. You two would make a handsome couple. I assume he's your old high school flame—your first true love—who you ran into at the storage facility yesterday."

I don't admit that he was my first and only. Instead, I give her a look. "Don't start playing matchmaker. We've agreed to be friends. We could both use one."

Blossom smiles, knowingly. "Friends for now, Daisy. The heart has a way of making its own plans."

"No way, Blossom! I refuse to make the same mistake twice."

Blossom lays a hand lightly on my shoulder. "You didn't make the mistake, Daisy. He did. He just didn't realize it until it was too late."

As I stand there, I'm struck by a sudden realization. Maybe losing him wasn't the end of anything. Maybe it was the beginning of becoming who I was meant to be. Maybe—just maybe—the best parts are still ahead of me.

Twelve

Sadie and I spend several hours on Saturday morning sorting through the contents of my storage unit. She has a remarkable knack for interior design, suggesting furniture for rooms I never even imagined. She circles each piece like she's auditioning it for a starring role. A forgotten armchair becomes the centerpiece of a reading nook. A narrow console I always thought was useless is suddenly perfect for the upstairs hallway. Her instinct is uncanny—quiet, confident, and completely unpretentious.

"With your eye for design, I'm surprised you didn't follow in your mother's footsteps," I say.

Sadie snorts. "Not a chance. I could never deal with her clients—rich women with zero taste who talk down to her like she's their housekeeper. Nothing's ever good enough. She's always redoing custom orders because someone doesn't like it. Or they claim she made a mistake. But somehow, Mom loves it. She thrives on it. She's in magazines all the time."

"Really? That's cool!" Then again, this highly successful designer can't be that great if she turned her back on her daughter when she needed her the most.

Sadie inspects a white porcelain lamp. "Does this have a mate?"

I shake my head. "No. Unfortunately."

"Too bad—they'd be perfect on your nightstands." She sets the lamp down, then picks it up again. "Let's keep it. We can use it on a chest or something in your bedroom," she says, adding the lamp to the growing pile we've set aside for the house.

By the time the movers arrive, I'm starting to worry it won't all fit. But the resourceful young men handle each item with care, their truck a giant puzzle where every piece finds its perfect place.

It's early afternoon when we finally make it back to the house. The front yard looks like we're holding a giant yard sale with Cash and Colby hauling out the pieces of Flossie's furniture I've decided to move into storage. I stand back, taking it all in, the familiar furnishings scattered across the lawn like fragments of a life I'm not quite ready to let go.

By late afternoon, the swap is complete, and I send the movers off with a generous tip and my heartfelt thanks.

I roam through the house, admiring the transformation from Flossie's domain to mine. Although it still feels like home, the edges have softened. The rooms are lighter now, the walls no longer shouting but speaking in calm, measured tones. The house no longer feels frozen in time. It feels like it's learning how to breathe again.

Gone are the gilded mirrors and jewel-toned drama. The long, formal dining-room table Flossie once insisted on has been replaced with a round one—smaller, more forgiving. The kind of table where no one sits at the head.

Flossie's presence still lingers—polished banister, meticulously maintained random-width oak floors, and her priceless collection of Audubons. But little by little, my touches are taking hold. The black-lacquered Chinese mirror looks striking above her antique console table in the hallway. In Dad's study, my teal velvet love seat adds a vibrant pop of color, anchoring the room alongside my Queen Anne desk and a geometric wool rug I'd forgotten I owned. It's no longer Dad's study—it's mine now. Quieter. Softer. A reflection of who I've become. I can almost picture it—decades of life unfolding in this room: grading papers, paying bills, maybe even writing the novel I always said I would.

Exhausted and ready to call it a night, I pull myself away from the study and head for the stairs. I pause in the living room doorway when I notice Sadie standing at the mantel, her gaze fixed on the purple urn.

When she sees me, she lifts the urn with one hand and holds it out. "What is this?"

I freeze, my eyes locked on the porcelain vessel, silently praying she doesn't drop it. "That's Flossie."

She giggles. "I figured it must've been hers. Definitely not your style. But why is it still here? I thought we sent all the Flossie rejects to storage."

I cross the room quickly, taking the urn from her hands and cradling it against my chest like something sacred. "It's not just Flossie's urn," I say softly. "It *is* Flossie. Her ashes are inside."

Sadie's hand flies to her mouth. "Oh my gosh, Selwyn. I'm so sorry. I didn't mean to be disrespectful. That was incredibly thoughtless of me."

"You didn't know. And for the record, this isn't the urn I picked out—the funeral home had a mix-up," I say, suddenly feeling the need to let this stylish young woman know I hadn't chosen the purple jug. I glance around the room. "I need to find a safer spot to keep it until I'm ready to scatter her ashes. Flossie would never forgive me if she wound up in a vacuum cleaner." I chuckle, imagining the look my mother would give me.

I move to the bookcases and carefully place the urn high up, out of reach.

Sadie watches me, still appearing stricken. "Where are you going to scatter her ashes?"

I hesitate—then realize the answer is already there, solid and sure inside me. "In the garden, after we finish restoring it."

The decision was never mine. Flossie decided. *And spread my ashes over a place of your choosing. Somewhere beautiful. Somewhere fragrant.*

Blossom was right. Flossie's soul has gone to heaven. Her ashes should return to the earth she loved so fiercely. Even if I sell the house one day, Flossie will live forever inside my heart —no matter where my feet land.

Sadie steps up beside me. "I didn't know her, but I'm sure she would've loved that. You're lucky you had such a close relationship with your mom." Her voice is wistful, clearly thinking of her own mother.

I smile over at her. "Were you ever close with your mom? You know, before this . . ." My gaze falls to her baby bump.

"Always. That's what makes this so hard. I never let her down before. Always made the dean's list, never got into trouble." She pauses, her voice quiet. "I guess it takes a crisis to see a person's true nature."

"Give her some time. She may come around," I say, though I have no idea if it's true.

"Maybe." Sadie turns away from the bookcases toward the now-empty space over the mantel. "You know . . . now that the urn is in a safe place, you could hang a flat-screen TV up there. Might make the living room feel a little less formal." She gives me a tentative smile. "Just a thought."

I laugh under my breath. "Flossie would've hated that." But the more I picture it, the more the idea grows on me. Maybe it wasn't what Flossie would've wanted, but a television would bring life back to this room. Messier, louder, more real. Flossie was always the center of attention in here—the showpiece, the storyteller, the spark. Maybe it's time the room found a new kind of heartbeat.

"I love it," I say finally. "I'll call the electrician on Monday."

Blossom glides into the room like she's been listening all along. "A television is just what this room needs! Hallmark movies and football—it'll be perfect." She pulls a tape measure from her dress pocket with a flourish. "Let's get a big one."

Ten minutes later, I'm standing on a stepladder, measuring for the television, when the front doorbell rings—followed by a familiar voice. "Hello? Anyone home?"

"In here," I call out.

Griffin appears in the doorway with a stack of pizza boxes balanced in his arms. "Anyone hungry?"

Sadie springs off the sofa. "That's a stupid question to ask a pregnant woman!"

The sound of our laughter fills the house in a way it hasn't in a long, long time.

We gather around the kitchen table with paper plates, napkins, and the pizza boxes. Sadie polishes off two slices before deciding she's cold.

"I'm going to run upstairs for a sweater," she says, pushing back from the table. Her footsteps on the stairs are soon followed by a scream. "Selwyn! Come quick."

The three of us rush upstairs to find Sadie in the nursery, clutching the crib railing.

"What is it?" I ask, hurrying to her side.

Inside the crib lies a delicate christening gown, its intricate lace slightly yellowed with age, spread out like a whispered blessing from the past.

My breath catches. "That's my christening gown."

Sadie turns to me, a trembling hand pressed against her

mouth. "Where did it come from? I didn't see any boxes of baby clothes in the storage unit."

"It must have been in the attic." I swallow hard. "But the bigger question is—who brought it down and put it here?" A chill runs through me, and I instinctively lean into Blossom. "This has to stop," I say, my voice low and tight.

Blossom's arm slips around my back, steadying me.

Griffin frowns, eyes darting between us. "What has to stop?"

"Yeah," Sadie echoes, her voice uncertain. "What's going on?"

I take a shaky breath and spill everything—the drawings, the rearranged objects, the things that keep vanishing. Everything except the pill bottle.

"Someone is stalking me. I don't know who or why, but they seem to know an awful lot about me."

Blossom reaches into the crib and gently lifts the christening gown. Beneath it lies another drawing—this one of the four of us, gathered around the kitchen table, just as we were only moments ago.

My stomach drops. I jab a finger at the drawing. "That just happened. Someone is watching us. Right now!" I turn to Blossom, my heart pounding. "Do you think it's time to call the police?"

She doesn't answer right away. Her gaze lingers on the drawing in her hand, then drifts to the christening gown draped over the side of the crib. "Maybe," she says at last. "But whoever this is—they haven't hurt anyone. Yet." She folds the drawing with practiced calm. "They're watching, yes. But it doesn't feel threatening. To me, it still feels personal. Maybe even . . . protective."

"Protective?" I echo. "Blossom, they placed my baby gown in a crib and drew us eating pizza. That's not protective. That's obsessive. And deeply unsettling."

Sadie edges closer to me, her face pale. "I think we should call the police," she whispers. "What if they try to come inside?"

I don't say the obvious—I don't want to scare her. But whoever it is has already been inside. Up in the attic. Spying on us eating pizza. In this very room, arranging the christening gown.

Blossom turns to her, her expression gentle. "I understand, honey. And if anything feels threatening, we'll call right away. But maybe give it one more day—just enough time to see if whoever's behind this steps forward. Sometimes when you shine a light, the shadows scatter. Sometimes . . . they come closer."

A chill ripples through me, but for Sadie's sake, I force myself to remain calm.

Griffin clears his throat, shifting awkwardly by the door. "I can check the locks and lights before I leave."

"That'd be great," I say, my voice tighter than I intend. "Thank you."

"And I'll sleep in the guest room if it makes you feel better," Blossom offers.

I nod. "Yes! Please."

We file back downstairs in silence. The kitchen still smells faintly of pizza, half-finished glasses of tea abandoned on the table. Sadie sinks into a chair, pulling a throw blanket over her lap, her eyes flickering nervously to the windows. Blossom gathers our paper plates and throws them in the trash, her every movement a calm reassurance as she tidies up.

The house feels different now. Tense. Breathing shallowly. As if it, too, is waiting.

Blossom catches my eye across the room, her voice low but firm. "Don't worry, Daisy. We'll figure it out. Just stay close to the people who love you."

I glance at Sadie, shivering beneath the throw, and at Blossom, steady as a rock. Even Griffin, fiddling with the deadbolt on the back door, seems to belong here now. I'm not alone anymore.

Still, the thought slips in before I can stop it. *I barely know any of them.*

Griffin and I have history, sure, but time doesn't equal trust. What do I really know about the man he is now? Blossom radiates warmth, but she also claims to be an angel. What if she's not divine, but delusional? And Sadie . . . just days ago, she was a stranger. Now she's curled under a blanket, one hand resting protectively on her belly. She looks innocent. But so did I, once.

Someone placed that gown in the crib. Drew us at this very table. Not one of us left the room. So, who did it? And more terrifying—why? And where are they now?

$$Thirteen$$

Retiring to my room, I pause to take in the space I've begun to make my own. The soft glow of the white porcelain lamp on Flossie's antique tall chest. My oversized chair and ottoman tucked beneath the brass floor lamp, forming a cozy reading nook in the corner. The faint, familiar scent of lavender lingers in the air—Flossie's old linen spray. And the quiet. All of it soothes me. For now, the comfort of the room softens my fears. Hopefully, tomorrow will bring answers.

As I turn back the bedcovers, I notice a dim light and flicker of movement in the garage apartment window. My gaze drifts to the garden below, and when I look up again, the window is dark. I'm imagining things. The *Watcher* is getting to me, setting my nerves on end.

A sudden memory surfaces—Flossie's funeral, the day I led the medical supply crew to the garage and we found the mildewed sofa. We'd heard a loud crash from above. Could that have been the *Watcher* even then?

First thing tomorrow, I tell myself. *Blossom and I will check out the apartment together.*

But when I wake during the night and spot a light burning

brightly in the apartment window, I can't wait any longer. I have to know who the *Watcher* is.

Slipping on my robe, I grab my phone from the bedside table, pad down the hall, and tap lightly on the guest bedroom door. "Blossom," I whisper loudly. "I'm sorry to bother you, but I think someone is living in my garage apartment."

The door cracks open. Blossom steps out, serene as ever—an angel in a gauzy white gown, her silver-streaked hair unbound, cascading down her shoulders like moonlight.

She meets my eyes, then nods with quiet resolve. "I'll fetch my slippers."

We're halfway down the stairs when it hits me. "What if whoever's been living in the apartment isn't the harmless soul you think they are? They've been watching me, Blossom—stalking me. We could be walking into a trap. Maybe we should call the police, let them check it out first."

Blossom exhales slowly, considering. "You're probably right."

I pull out my phone and punch in the numbers.

"911, what's your emergency?" a woman answers in a nasal tone.

I give her my name and a quick rundown of the situation.

"I'll send someone over right away. Would you like to stay on the phone until an officer arrives?"

"No, ma'am. We'll be fine waiting in the house. But please —ask them not to come in with sirens blaring. I don't want to alarm my neighbors."

"Understood."

Five minutes later, flashing blue lights strobe through the kitchen window. To their credit, the sirens are off. Blossom and I hurry outside to greet them.

A female officer steps out of the cruiser. "Evening, ma'am. I'm Officer Marla Quinn. I understand you've got a squatter?"

I nod tightly. "I think so. Strange things have been

happening—drawings, items moved or missing. Just a few minutes ago, I noticed a light on upstairs." I point toward the second floor of the garage.

"You wait inside while I take a look," Officer Quinn says, unclipping her flashlight from her belt.

Despite her instruction, Blossom and I trail behind at a distance, climbing the narrow staircase that hugs the side of the garage. The wooden steps groan beneath our feet.

At the top, Officer Quinn raps on the door with the butt of her flashlight. "Police! Open up!"

"It's unlocked," comes a muffled voice from within.

Quinn pushes the door open and sweeps her light through the apartment's sitting room. Dust particles dance in the beam, but the space is unexpectedly clean. Tidy. Someone's been here. Recently. Then the light finds her.

A figure—small, feminine—curled in the far corner behind the sofa. Knees drawn to her chest, face half-hidden beneath a tangle of curls.

Officer Quinn kneels beside her, lowering her voice. "And who do we have here? What's your name, sweetheart?"

The girl flinches, shrinking deeper into the corner. "Alice Jones. Please don't take me to jail."

"I'm not here to arrest you," Quinn says in a low, reassuring voice. "But you are trespassing on private property."

Alice's chin quivers. "But I don't have anywhere else to go. Please, let me stay. I promise I won't bother anybody."

"That's not my decision. Come on. Let's get you up." Quinn takes her by the arm and lifts her to her feet.

She looks about twenty, but there's a strange youthfulness to her—something unformed, almost childlike. And her eyes —wide and clear—sparkle like uncut diamonds.

I step farther into the apartment, studying her more closely. There's something about her . . . something familiar.

Then I remember. "I saw you at my mother's funeral. You were across the room. And—just like that—you vanished."

Alice recoils but doesn't deny it.

I shake my head in confusion. "What's going on here? Who are you?" I ask, my voice now tinged with anger.

Blossom rests a hand on my shoulder. "Why don't we go inside? I'll make us a pot of coffee."

I shoot her a look. "Coffee? It's either too early or too late for that. What time is it anyway?"

Officer Quinn glances at her watch. "Just past five."

I exhale. "Then I guess it's morning. Fine. Let's make some coffee. Because I want to hear Alice's story. I want to know why she's been stalking me."

We descend the stairs in single file—me, Blossom, Alice, with Officer Quinn bringing up the rear—and make our way through the garden to the house.

In the kitchen, Blossom moves with quiet purpose, filling the quiet with the clink of mugs and the low hum of the coffeemaker.

The rest of us gather at the table. I sit across from Alice, unable to look away. There's something arresting about her— yes, she's beautiful, but it's more than that. There's a pull I can't explain. A connection I don't understand.

Officer Quinn opens her tablet. "Your family must be worried about you. Is there someone we can call?"

Alice shakes her head. "I don't have any family."

"No one?" Quinn presses. "What about your parents?"

"My mother left when I was little. My father died a few years ago."

"Any siblings?"

Alice chews her lower lip but stays silent.

Blossom sets steaming mugs in front of us, her movements unhurried. "How old are you, Alice?"

"Twenty," she says, straightening slightly. "Old enough to be on my own."

"To be on your own, you need to support yourself." Quinn takes a mug and blows on the coffee. "Are you working?"

Alice doesn't answer. Instead, she looks straight at me. "If you let me stay, I can help around the house. Do laundry. Babysit Sadie's baby. Even grade papers."

That catches me off guard. "Grade papers? You do know I teach at the college level."

Alice blushes and drops her gaze. "I'm smart. At least . . . that's what people used to say."

There's a beat of silence before Officer Quinn asks gently, "Are you on the spectrum, Alice?"

Alice lifts one shoulder. "Somewhere. They never really figured out where I fit."

I glance at her, confused. "Who's they?"

Her mouth tightens. She doesn't answer.

I shift gears. "Where were you living before this?"

"A long way from here."

"And how did you end up in Oxford?" I ask.

She hesitates, then says, "A lady brought me."

Quinn sets her mug down with a soft clink. "Did you know her?"

Alice fidgets. "Not really. She was just . . . someone who helped me."

"A stranger?" Quinn presses.

Alice picks at a thread on her sleeve, her gaze fixed on the table. "I don't know. Maybe. I told her I needed to get here, and she brought me."

"Why here? Why Oxford?" I ask. "It's not exactly a place you stumble into."

Alice stares down into her coffee like it might answer for her. Finally, in a voice barely above a whisper, she says,

"Someone used to read Faulkner to me. Said Oxford was sacred ground. I guess I wanted to see it for myself."

This resonates with me. My father used to call Faulkner *the voice of the South*. He never taught me to ride a bike, but he read Faulkner's more poetic passages aloud to me, letting the words hang in the air like incense. He taught me to love language.

"Most people your age wouldn't touch Faulkner," I say, a smile tugging at my mouth. "I'd be happy to give you the Faulkner tour."

Alice's face lights up. "Really? That'd be great. Does this mean I can stay?"

"Maybe." I push back from the table and retrieve the drawings from the drawer beside the back door, setting them in front of her. "First, you need to explain these."

Alice glances down at them, then up at me—grinning from ear to ear like a delighted child. "Do you like them?"

"Yes, of course. You're very talented." I ease back into my chair, studying her. "But why have you been following me?"

"Because you're so pretty. And you seem so nice. I wanted to know more about you."

I try not to react—though, truthfully, I'm flattered. "Why did you take my mother's phone?"

"I wanted to see the pictures of the garden," she says simply. "To make sure you were replanting it right. I moved a few things around, by the way. I hope you don't mind. I don't think you even noticed."

I glance at Blossom, who looks positively enchanted. "I noticed," she says with a soft chuckle. "I thought I'd done it. I was starting to question my memory. I'm glad to know it was you."

Turning back to Alice, I ask, "And the books in my father's study? Why did you swap some of his for mine?"

Alice sits up straighter, suddenly composed. "I was

encouraging you to use the space. The makeover looks great, by the way. The white paint gives it a clean palette for you to create."

I can't help but smile. One minute she's all impish curiosity, the next she's talking like a design student at SCAD.

"I'm glad you like it." I tap the paint chip on the table. "And this?"

Alice waves a hand airily. "Just letting you know I approve. *Balboa Mist* sounds so exotic—like a place where artists wear linen and drink espresso by the sea."

"It does, doesn't it?" I lean in, my voice dropping. "And the pills?"

Her smile falters. "I flushed them," she says softly. "You were so upset. I know you didn't mean to hurt yourself. I'm the one who ordered the pizza that night. The delivery guy came to the wrong door. Maybe his timing wasn't so wrong after all."

I sit with that for a beat. The delivery guy may have saved my life—though I want to believe I wouldn't have gone through with it. "Maybe," I murmur.

"Can I stay, Selwyn? Pretty please." She clasps her hands in mock prayer, her clear eyes wide with hope.

I chew on a hangnail. "What do you think?" I ask, glancing at Blossom.

She lifts her coffee mug with a wry smile. "That's up to you, Daisy. But you've already got one stranger living in the house. What's one more?"

Alice pops halfway out of her chair. "Yay! You won't be sorry. I promise."

My hand shoots out, halting her mid-bounce. "Hang on. Before you celebrate—there will be rules. And you'll have to respect my privacy."

"I understand," Alice says, nodding enthusiastically, her white-blonde curls dancing like a loose halo.

Officer Quinn rises from her seat. "I'll need to file a report. I assume you won't be pressing any charges?"

"No. We're good. But thank you for coming. And I'm sorry for the false alarm."

She grins. "Are you kidding me? This is the most fun I've had in weeks." She turns to Alice, wagging a finger. "You listen to Selwyn now. Do what she says."

"Yes, ma'am," Alice replies, suddenly solemn.

Quinn hands each of us a business card. "I hope you don't need me, but if you do, call me directly."

I get up and walk her to the door. "Are you going to investigate? She obviously came from somewhere. Someone has to be missing her."

Quinn pauses, her hand on the doorknob. "Do you *want* me to investigate? If she escaped from a residential care facility, they may insist she be returned. But I don't know . . ." She glances back toward the table. "There's something about the two of you—like you were meant to cross paths. Like two people who have both suffered loss and need each other to heal."

I nod slowly. It feels like more than that, but Alice won't talk until she's ready. "Maybe make some indiscreet inquiries. Quiet ones."

Quinn nods once. "I can do that."

I close the door behind her and return to the table. "Let's hope I don't end up on some watchlist for harboring wayward souls."

Blossom sets her mug down with a thoughtful clunk. "You could hang a shingle out front that says *Welcome to the Porchlight Inn—where the light's always on and the misfits find their way home.*"

Alice claps her hands like she's just heard the name of a fairytale. "I love it!"

Sadie slouches into the room, one hand over her mouth to

stifle a yawn. "What're y'all doing up so early?" She stops short at the sight of Alice. "And who are you?"

"Alice Jones," she says brightly. "Latest addition to the Porchlight Inn—house for misfits."

Sadie blinks. "It's way too early for me to understand that. Especially when I can't drink coffee."

"Alice has been living in the garage apartment," I explain. "She's the friendly ghost who put out the christening gown. She's going to be staying with us for a while." I look over at Alice. "Would you like to move into the house?"

She shakes her head. "I'd rather stay in the apartment, if you don't mind. I cleaned it up. It's nice and cozy. I could use some towels and washcloths though."

I smile. "We have plenty of those. You can stay out there for now. But I don't want you out late at night."

Alice nods quickly. "Oh, don't worry. I'm not allowed out at night at Waverly."

The words land oddly—like they've slipped through a crack in time. I glance at her, but she's already looking away, like it's nothing. Still, it chills me. Who taught her that? Who enforced it? Where did this girl come from? What and where is Waverly?

I clear my throat. "On that note, I'm going back to bed until it's time to get ready for church. If anyone would like to join me, I'm treating to brunch afterward at Big Bad Breakfast."

Alice lights up. "Church and brunch? I've never done that before." Then, she slips her hand into mine—for just a second, but long enough to say everything. "I'd like that," she says, almost in a whisper.

The contact is fleeting, but it hits me deep—a tender place I didn't know was still exposed. I'm not sure what's happening to me. I'm falling head over heels in love with this girl. Not the romantic kind of love. I prefer men for that. This is something else entirely—fierce, protective, aching to matter.

Maybe this is what it feels like to be found.

Fourteen

Over fluffy biscuits and bottomless coffee at Big Bad Breakfast, Alice turns her full attention to Sadie, firing off questions about the baby like an eager reporter on a deadline.

Blossom sips her tea with a bemused smile. I watch, equal parts entertained and awestruck, my fork paused in midair. But Sadie—clearly as taken with Alice as the rest of us— answers each question with quiet grace and surprising patience, like a big sister who's already decided this girl belongs to her.

When Alice asks why Sadie isn't marrying her baby daddy, she responds, "Because he hasn't asked."

Alice bites into a chicken biscuit. "But what if he *does* ask?" she says, mouth half full.

"I don't think he will," Sadie replies, forking off a bite of avocado toast.

Alice stops chewing. "But your baby needs a daddy, Sadie."

Sadie lowers her gaze, shaking her head. "Not a daddy who is forced into being involved in his child's life."

"Are you in love with him?"

"I thought I was. Once. But I was wrong about him. Jake's not the person I thought . . . or hoped he was."

Jake. His name is Jake. I've asked Sadie several times about the baby's father. But she never gave me a name. Somehow, Alice gets people to open up—without even trying. It's like she coaxes the truth out of them before they realize they've said too much.

Alice tilts her head. "But what if he changes his mind about marrying you? I could talk to him, if you want."

Sadie gives the girl a sad smile. "That's sweet of you, Alice. And I appreciate your concern. But he's starting law school at Georgetown in the fall. He doesn't have time for a wife and baby."

Alice props her elbows on the table, resting her chin in her hands. "What about your parents? Maybe they'll change their minds and help you out."

"I'm not holding my breath. They're pretty mad at me." Sadie's face is twisted in pain. I can see how much she's hurting—how much she's trying not to let it show.

"Let me think on it. I'll figure something out." Alice crunches on a slice of bacon. "So . . . what're we doing for the rest of the day?"

"I'm writing a paper for my summer school class," Sadie volunteers.

"Ooh. I can write it for you!" Alice says, eyes bright.

Sadie giggles. "That would be cheating, Alice."

Alice's shoulders sag. "I guess you're right." She looks over at me. "Can I do the assignment too, just for fun?"

I start to say no—it's college-level work—but then I realize it's the perfect opportunity to test her intellect. "I don't see why not. You can borrow my copy of *As I Lay Dying*. After reading the book, write a three-to-five-page paper exploring Faulkner's use of interior monologue, perspective, and voice to develop character and reveal deeper truths—or contradictions—about identity, grief, and family obligation."

Alice appears undeterred by my technical jargon. "That sounds intriguing. I'll get right on it when we get home. What're you doing this afternoon, Selwyn?"

I glance over at Blossom. "Are we gardening?"

"Yes, ma'am," Blossom says with a grin. "The compost is ready, and we need to get it worked into the soil before the mulch arrives tomorrow."

Alice's hand shoots up. "I'll help."

I raise an eyebrow. "But what about your assignment?"

"Duh. I can do both. I have all afternoon."

I can't help but laugh. "You are full of surprises, Alice Jones."

As we finish up brunch, I sip the last of my coffee and glance out the window at the clear sky. A perfect day for planting.

The garden is nearly complete—beds edged, new plants in the ground, roses pruned. I should be thrilled the project is coming to an end and that I can soon scatter Flossie's ashes. But does this mean Blossom will be leaving? I hate how tightly I've come to rely on her presence—her quiet strength, her knowing looks, the way she hums when she works.

If only my guardian angel could stay forever.

By early afternoon, we're back at the house, changed into gardening clothes. Blossom's already out back, spreading compost with a dirt rake, the brim of her sunhat casting a shadow over her eyes.

I grab another rake and begin smoothing compost nearby.

"Will you disappear when we finish this garden?" I ask lightly, hoping the question lands as casual. But my heart's in my throat.

"Not yet," Blossom says, raking in even purposeful

strokes. "I came to help you find direction in your life. My work here is not finished."

"But I've found that direction," I say, thinking how far I've come in only a week.

"You've found two people to share your home. There's no guarantee how long they'll stay here. You can't live for other people, Daisy. You've been doing that for the past six years with your parents."

"But helping people *is* my new direction. If—when—Alice and Sadie move on, I'll find someone new to help. I work at a university with over twenty thousand students. There will always be someone in need."

"What you're doing is admirable. As long as there's something for *you* in it." Blossom pauses, leaning on her rake. "You've got a big heart, Daisy. And that's a gift—but it can be a burden, too, if you're not careful. Be sure the people you help aren't just passing through your life to take what they need."

I look over at her, startled. "You think that's what Alice and Sadie are doing?"

She smiles, soft but unreadable. "I think they're here for a reason. Just don't forget—you are too."

I rake in silence for a while, letting Blossom's words settle. *As long as there's something for you in it.*

It's the kind of thing that sounds simple. But it isn't.

I want to believe helping others is enough. That offering this home, this patch of steadiness, is purpose enough. But Blossom sees through me. And maybe she's right. Maybe it's not just about what I'm giving. Maybe it's time to start thinking about what I need too.

Late afternoon, I'm working in my study, prepping lectures for the week, when Alice taps lightly on the porch door and pokes her head inside. "Am I interrupting?"

"Not at all. Come on in," I say, waving her in.

She crosses the room and stands in front of my desk. "I finished the assignment, but I don't have a printer. I emailed you the Word document."

I glance at the brass clock that once belonged to my father—one of the few things of his I've kept. "You read *As I Lay Dying* and wrote a paper in just under four hours?"

Alice shrugs. "It was really good. I enjoyed it."

"You actually enjoyed *As I Lay Dying*? You truly are an enigma, Alice. I wish the rest of my students felt the same."

Alice fidgets with her hands. "So, you'll print it and grade it for me? I want to know what you think."

"Of course. I can't wait to read your thoughts."

She moves to the doorway, peeks into the hallway, then gently closes the door. From her shorts pocket, she pulls out a rolled scroll tied with a yellow satin ribbon. "I've been thinking . . . we should throw Sadie a surprise baby shower. I made a list of the things she'll need for the baby." She unties the ribbon and unrolls the list. "Basically? She needs everything. But we can just start with the basics."

I lean back in my chair, smiling despite myself. "It's not a bad idea. But who would we invite? All her friends have moved on to the next chapter of their lives."

Alice ticks names off her fingers. "You, me, Blossom, Rosa, Griffin . . ."

I freeze. "You know Rosa?"

Her cheeks flush. "I mean, I've never actually *met* her. But I've seen her around. We should have the shower next Saturday, just in case the baby comes early. She doesn't have a registry—I checked. I think we should just buy her what we want her to have."

I laugh out loud. "Why not?" Saturday is my birthday. None of my new friends know this. I doubt Rosa remembers. And Flossie isn't here to celebrate. We'll have a baby shower instead.

"Yippee," Alice says, doing a victory dance around my study, arms flailing, curls bouncing. "If you'll invite everyone, I'll work on the decorations."

"Deal." I smile to myself. This will give me a reason to call Griffin.

She starts out of the door and then spins back around. "Oh! I almost forgot. I made a shopping list for you too," she says, pulling an identical scroll from her pocket and tossing it to me.

As she flits away, light on her feet and brimming with purpose, I think maybe—just maybe—this birthday won't be so bad after all.

Fifteen

I'm speechless after reading Alice's paper. Her insight into Faulkner's layered narration and shifting points of view is more intuitive than anything I've encountered from my most gifted students. It's obvious she's on the spectrum, but she's highly functional in ways that matter deeply—intellectually, creatively, perceptively. While she struggles with social filters and boundaries, I've yet to witness a single challenge that would prevent her from living independently. I'd love to see what she could accomplish with the right opportunities. I want her to have the chance to reach her full potential. Maybe I'll speak to the head of the English department about letting her audit a class or two this fall. If all goes well, she could enroll full-time in the spring.

Here I go again—making plans for people I hardly know. Blossom's words echo in my mind. *Be sure the people you help aren't just passing through your life to take what they need.*

I pick up my phone and tap on Griffin's number.

"Selwyn!" he answers, sounding surprised. "I wasn't expecting to hear from you. What're you up to this Sunday evening?"

"I'm calling to invite you to a baby shower. And before you shut me down, hear me out—it's not your typical baby shower. I have a new resident staying in my house of wayward souls—the Porchlight Inn we're calling it, where the light's always on and the misfits find their way home."

Griffin chuckles. "I'm intrigued. Tell me more about this newest misfit."

"Her name is Alice Jones. She's the one who's been following me, rearranging things, making things disappear. She's . . . something else. But I'll let you see for yourself. She's determined to throw Sadie a baby shower, and since all Sadie's college friends have cleared out of Oxford, I'm scrambling for warm bodies. For the record, inviting you was Alice's idea. Even though you two have never met, she talks about you like you're old friends. You don't need to bring a gift or anything."

"Stop, Selwyn!" he says, his voice warm. "You don't have to convince me. I'd love to come."

"Great! We'll have fun." I give him the logistics, and we talk for a minute more before hanging up.

I sit quietly, scrolling through Alice's list. She wasn't kidding—Sadie needs everything. How could one tiny human require so much gear? And poor Sadie doesn't have a cent to her name. I make a mental reminder to properly sort the list tomorrow and place a big order on Amazon.

But the next morning, while packing up for work, I spot my laptop still open on my desk—my Amazon cart filled with several hundred dollars' worth of baby gear. Unless I've developed the ability to shop in my sleep, Alice has taken matters into her own hands.

I groan. First, coffee.

Tossing my tote over my shoulder, I head to the kitchen and find Alice and Rosa talking in hushed tones, heads tilted close.

"If I didn't know better," I say, eyeing them both, "I'd think you two knew each other from before."

Alice's cheeks flush bright pink. "Umm . . ."

Rosa straightens, casually brushing crumbs off the counter. "Nope. We just met. We were talking about the baby shower. Lots to plan." She glances over at Alice, and something passes between them—a flicker? Something I can't quite put my finger on. But it lingers too long to ignore.

"Mm-hmm," I say, giving them a skeptical look, just enough to let them know I'm not buying it.

Setting my tote on the counter, I pull out my laptop and wave it at Alice. "You promised to stop sneaking around. And that includes using my laptop without asking. Why didn't you use your own to shop for the baby shower?"

Alice gives a sheepish shrug. "Because you're the one buying. I don't have any money."

I sigh, setting down the laptop. "I'm happy to pay for the shower gifts, but do you really not have *any* money?"

"Nope. Not a cent."

How did I end up with two freeloaders and a baby on the way? *Welcome to the Porchlight Inn, where the light's always on and no one pays rent.*

I pull Alice's assignment from my tote and hand it to her, a large A+ written in red marker across the top. "I printed your paper. This is excellent."

Beaming, she sits up straight. "Really? Can I do some more assignments?"

"Sure. And if you don't mind, I'd like to keep this one. I want to show it to the head of my department. How would you feel about taking some classes next fall?"

She bounces on the stool like a child at Christmas. "Are you kidding? I'd love it! Can I join a sorority?"

Before I can respond, Sadie waddles into the kitchen wearing a T-shirt from her old sorority stretched snug over her baby bump. "Alice in a sorority?" she mutters, reaching for the coffeepot. "God help the Greek system."

Alice grins, undeterred. "What? I think I'd look cute in letters."

Sadie pours her coffee, eyes narrowed in amusement. "You'd definitely shake things up. Maybe start your own— Delta House of Misfits."

Rosa laughs out loud. "I'd pledge."

I shake my head. "On that note, I'm off to class," I say, snatching the paper from Alice and stuffing it in my tote.

On my drive over to the university, I think about how drastically my life has changed since Flossie's funeral. Some days, I feel more like a housemother for a sorority than a literature professor. Truth be told, I wouldn't have it any other way.

Later that afternoon, Sadie and I are backing out of the driveway, headed to tour the hospital's birthing center, when Alice darts out the back door and knocks on my window.

"Wait for me!" she calls, climbing into the back seat and buckling up. "I can't wait to see the babies. Aren't you excited, Sadie?"

Sadie rolls her eyes. "Thrilled."

Her response surprises me. There's a sharpness behind the sarcasm that gives me pause. Is she nervous about the delivery? Or maybe it's something more . . . Maybe she's tired of Alice tagging along—of suddenly having to share the spotlight in a moment that should feel personal and sacred. I wouldn't blame her. The closer she gets to meeting this baby, the more real everything becomes. And real has a way of stirring up all the things we thought we'd figured out.

My suspicions are confirmed on Wednesday afternoon when Sadie texts me. She's upstairs working on an assignment, and I'm in my study grading papers.

I'm nervous about my doctor's
appointment. Will you please go with me?

I respond right away.

Of course. What time?

Four. Can we meet at her office? I'd rather
Alice not come along this time.

I hesitate for a second before typing: *I understand.*

Two hours later, as we sit in the waiting room, flipping through outdated magazines, I glance over at Sadie, her foot bouncing nervously.

"I hope you don't mind me asking," I say carefully. "Is everything okay between you and Alice?"

Sadie sighs, closing her magazine and dropping it on the table. "It's not Alice. She's sweet. But she's so excited about the baby. I feel like I have to pretend when I'm around her. I'm too afraid to be excited, Selwyn. I don't even know what my future looks like."

I reach over and give her hand a gentle squeeze. "I'm sure you are. And you're not alone. I have no idea what my future holds, and I'm not the one having a baby."

Sadie plucks at the threads in her ripped jeans. "Have you given up on your dream of having a baby? If you could have one now, would you want it?"

I shift in my seat, startled by the question. "That's a tough question, Alice. For years, I was obsessed with having a baby. But now? I guess I've made peace with the way things turned out. Life has a funny way of offering second chances—just not always in the form we expect."

Sadie looks away, blinking quickly. "Yeah. Funny how that works."

"You don't have to figure it all out right now. One step at a time, okay?"

The nurse appears, calling Sadie to the examining room. When Janey arrives, I step out into the hallway while she performs the pelvic exam. When Janey calls me back in a few minutes later, her brow is pinched in concern.

"Is everything okay?" I ask, returning to my seat.

"The baby is fine." Janey offers Sadie a reassuring smile. "You're fully effaced and dilated two centimeters. Your little one is eager to make his or her arrival into the world."

"But my due date isn't for two weeks," Sadie says, horror washing over her face. "I haven't even finished my class yet."

Janey chuckles. "Tell that to your baby." She leans against the counter. "But we have a bit of a problem. Your parents have canceled your health insurance. I'm willing to forgo my fees, but you'll still need to pay the hospital—and those expenses will be in the thousands."

The color drains from Sadie's face, and she bursts into tears —loud, gut-wrenching sobs that shake her shoulders. I have a hunch this isn't just about the hospital bill. This is about her parents rejecting her at the most vulnerable time in her life.

I rise from my chair and wrap an arm around her, rubbing soft circles on her back. "Don't worry, Sadie. We'll figure something out. I'll loan you the money, and you can pay me back whenever you're able."

"The hospital won't turn you away," Janey says with the kind of certainty that comes from having seen it all. "They offer financial assistance and payment plans. You'll be okay."

Sadie swipes at her eyes with the back of her hand. "I should be grateful, right? My parents paid for college. At least I won't have student loans in addition to this hospital debt." Her voice drips with sarcasm, but the pain beneath it is obvious. She inhales an unsteady breath. "I don't mean to take this out on you two. This is not your problem. You've both been so incredibly kind. I'll figure something out."

I smile at her. "You're not alone in this. We'll figure something out—together." Giving her shoulder a pat, I add, "Now, get dressed. I'll wait for you in the hallway."

Janey and I step out of the room, the door clicking softly shut behind us.

"Do you think the baby will come soon?" I ask.

Janey lifts her hands in a helpless *Who knows?* gesture. "Could be any day, or she could go another two weeks. It's hard to predict." She glances back toward the exam room, her expression softening. "I see girls like Sadie all the time. It breaks my heart. Their families turn their backs, the baby's father disappears, and they're left to navigate everything alone. Thankfully, the hospital does what it can, and there are some local charities that step in too."

"That's good to know. We'll do some investigating." I smile at my old friend. "I hate to ask when you've already done so much. But we're throwing Sadie a surprise shower on Saturday, and I would love for you to come. No gifts. Just stop by for a glass of wine if you can."

Janey shakes her head, her expression warm but apologetic. "I wish I could, Selwyn. Truly. But Jason has a baseball tournament in Memphis. We won't get back until late." She bumps my shoulder. "See what you're missing out on? All-day baseball tournaments. And you know how much I love baseball." She chuckles. "Not."

She means it as a joke, but it hits harder than I expect. I've always hated baseball, but I'd sit through a doubleheader in the blazing sun if it meant cheering on a child of my own.

Sadie is quiet on the drive home. I hear sniffling and suspect she's crying again. My heart aches for her, but I don't try to console her. She needs to cycle through these emotions on her own.

I'm surprised to find Griffin waiting in the driveway when we get home. Sadie waves at him but hurries inside without stopping.

"She's having a bad day," I explain. "She's under a lot of pressure."

"I can't imagine. Having a baby is tough enough when you're married. I'm glad you're having this shower for her—which is why I stopped by." He pulls out his phone. "I can't decide which stroller to get. These are my two top choices."

I glance down at his screen. "A stroller? Griffin, that's too much."

"No, it's not. Unless you've already bought one. Then I'll get her something else."

I mentally scroll through the list of baby gear Alice and I ordered from Amazon. "Nope. No stroller yet."

"Perfect. Then that's what I'll bring." He hands me his phone, and we spend a few minutes reviewing the two options.

He talks through the pros and cons like someone who's done his fair share of stroller duty. I can't help but wonder how many hours he spent pushing his own girls around the neighborhood.

"How about we have a cookout after the shower?" he suggests. "I'll bring burgers."

I smile. "That sounds lovely. Blossom and I will handle the sides."

As he heads back to his truck, I watch him go, feeling strangely grateful for his presence—his thoughtfulness, his easy way of showing up without needing to be asked.

I close the front door behind me and lean against it for a second, listening to the quiet hum of the house. I wonder if he remembers Saturday is my birthday. Some small part of me really hopes he does.

Sixteen

On Wednesday evening, us *Wayward Wonders* gather in the kitchen to prepare dinner. Sadie stands at the stove, watching Blossom blacken shrimp for tacos, trying to act normal but looking like she might unravel at any second. I catch myself watching her when she doesn't know I'm looking. There's a softness to her that's new—a vulnerability that clings to her like a second skin. It stirs something in me. A longing, maybe. Or a reckoning. I used to think I had nothing left to give. Now I wonder if I was simply waiting for the right people to give it to.

"How was your doctor's appointment?" Blossom asks in that knowing tone of hers, like she already suspects the answer but wants to hear it anyway.

"I'm fully effaced and dilated two centimeters," Sadie murmurs, casting a quick glance toward Alice.

She may be trying to keep it quiet, but there's no hiding anything from that inquisitive girl—not for long.

Sure enough, Alice looks up from pouring sweet tea into the glasses. "Seriously? That's amazing." She sets down the tea pitcher. "Are you exhibiting any symptoms? Cramping? Discharge? Pelvic pressure?" She glances at the door. "Obviously, your water hasn't broken, or we'd be tossing you in the car right now, on the way to the hospital."

Sadie shoots Alice a glare. "My only symptom is a sudden loss of appetite. If you'll excuse me, I think I'll pass on dinner." She turns away from the stove and flees the room.

Alice's face crumples, tears springing to her eyes. "Was it something I said? I have that effect on people sometimes. I don't mean to, but I open my mouth, and all the wrong words just spill out."

Blossom moves the skillet off the burner and sets the tongs aside. "Hush now, sweet child," she says, cupping the girl's face. "Don't take it to heart. Sadie's tender right now, understandably so. She's carrying a lot, and we need to respect her privacy. She'll share what she wants us to know when she's ready."

Alice nods, her chin quivering.

I marvel at how quickly Alice bounces back. By the time we sit down to eat, she's chattering nonstop again about the surprise shower. If only we all knew how to let things roll off our backs that easily.

For the next few days, Alice watches Sadie like a mother hen in training. I can see how hard it is for her not to pepper our expectant mama with questions, but she follows Blossom's advice in respecting her privacy.

As the packages arrive from Amazon, she meticulously wraps them in colorful paper and ribbons she claims she found in the attic. I don't doubt it. Flossie had a thing for elaborate wrapping paper.

Blossom is waiting in the garden when I arrive home from campus on Friday afternoon, her hands on her hips and a smudge of dirt on her cheek. "I'm proud to pronounce the restoration complete. Unless you have several hours a week to spare, you might consider hiring a gardener to maintain it."

"I can do that," I say. "Your friends at the garden center might be able to recommend someone."

Blossom nods. "I'm sure they can. Come. I have a surprise for you."

Taking me by the hand, she leads me to the herb section. Nestled in the lavender beds is a garden fairy. "A proper guardian for this garden," she says softly. "And a little reminder that Flossie's sass and sparkle still live on."

I gasp. "She's beautiful, Blossom. What a lovely addition to the garden."

I kneel to inspect her. She's no ordinary fairy—bold and bursting with color, made of hand-painted resin with delicate inlays of colored glass. Her wings shimmer in hues of teal, gold, and coral, like sunlit stained glass. Her dress is a swirl of vibrant florals—dahlias, zinnias, wild roses—sculpted into the folds of her skirt. She stands barefoot in a dancing pose, one foot lifted mid-twirl, arms outstretched in welcome. Her silver hair is swept into a loose chignon, a tiny watering can dangling from one hand. There's a mischievous twinkle in her painted eyes and a smile that says she knows all your secrets but loves you anyway.

I throw my arms around Blossom. "I don't know how to thank you. She's the perfect addition to the garden, a special gift I'll never forget. Not only will she remind me of Flossie— I'll think of you every time I see her." I pull back to study her face. "This sounds like goodbye. Are you leaving me?"

She thumbs my cheek. "Not a chance. With Sadie moodier than a cat in a rainstorm and Alice watching her like a teapot set to whistle, we're gonna need all hands on deck to get this baby born without someone losing their mind—or their manners."

I laugh. "You're right about that."

But when tears rise, I lower my gaze, the gravel driveway blurring beneath me. "I've been thinking a lot about what you said. I love helping others—it gives me a deep sense of purpose. But I need something that's mine alone. Something that fulfills me . . . in case the others leave—or when they do."

Blossom gently lifts my chin. "And you don't feel that way about teaching?"

"I used to, in the beginning, when my students seemed more engaged. If only I had more students like Sadie." I chuckle. "And Alice."

I step back from Blossom and gaze at the garden fairy. "There's a hollow place inside me," I whisper. "I don't know what's missing. Only that it is."

Blossom tilts her head, her emerald eyes filled with kindness. "People can fill a void, Daisy. But they shouldn't be expected to fill every crack. It doesn't always take a job or a passion project. Sometimes it's just letting yourself be seen. Letting someone love you back. Just make sure you're not always the one doing the giving. Whatever it is you find next— it needs to do more than fill your time. It needs to feed your soul."

"A baby would've done that," I say softly, then shrug. "Too late now."

She reaches out and smooths a strand of hair behind my ear, like she's done it a hundred times. "Some dreams go quiet, but that doesn't mean they're gone. Life has a funny way of sending us what we need, even if it shows up wearing a different name."

I swallow hard, unsure if it's her words or something deeper—something unspoken—that makes my chest tighten.

For years, I tried to bury the ache of the baby I never had, folding it neatly into the corners of my life like a letter I refused to read. But the longing never left. It lingered in empty rooms and echoing silences. But now that I've opened my house to Alice and Sadie—and with a baby on the way—that old longing is stirring again. Not the same shape, not the same dream, but familiar just the same. Maybe I wasn't meant to be a mother in the traditional sense. Maybe I was meant to love in a way that looks a little different.

Seventeen

Sadie holes up in her room, determined to finish her classwork before the baby arrives—like she's racing a clock only she can hear ticking. She skips meals with the rest of us, but I assume she's eating—sneaking down to the kitchen when the house is quiet. I try not to worry, giving her the space she seems to need. On the bright side, her absence makes it easier to pull together the surprise shower without raising suspicion.

Alice is beside herself, stringing streamers, blowing up balloons, arranging the gifts in a tidy little mountain. She's created games for us to play and invented a mocktail she calls *the Blush Bloom*, made with white peach juice, pink grapefruit juice, freshly squeezed lime juice, and a splash of elderflower syrup.

Everyone gathers at four, and Alice insists we all hide in the living room before I call Sadie downstairs. I have seen little of our expectant mama these past few days, and I'm startled by how pale she looks—dark circles smudged beneath her eyes, her shoulders slumped with exhaustion. Something's weighing on her. And it's more than the baby. More than being unmarried and broke.

When the others pop out of their hiding places, she startles, and the second she sees the mound of gifts, the tears come fast. "I can't believe you did this for me. It's too much. You're too good to me. I don't deserve it."

Blossom rushes to her side, wrapping her in a warm hug. "You most certainly do deserve it," she murmurs, her voice thick with emotion. "You need things for the baby, but more than that, you need to feel surrounded. Loved. We had the best time putting this together. Especially Alice. She's been counting down the days like it's Christmas morning."

Alice appears at her side, practically glowing. "Are you ready to open your presents?"

"I guess," Sadie murmurs, looking like she'd rather disappear into the woodwork.

Alice takes the lead, unwrapping most of the gifts while Sadie sits beside her, quietly observing. In addition to the basics—onesies, towels, and diapers—Alice and I have given a car seat, a bouncy seat, and a swing.

Griffin's stroller is a tremendous hit. Sadie actually gets up to hug him.

Rosa's gift is a hand-stitched baby quilt, sewn from fabric she's saved over the years.

Alice reads the note aloud. "Every square has a story. Some came from dresses I made for my daughter. Some from curtains that once hung in this very house that Miss Flossie donated to the cause. May it wrap your little one in warmth and love, always."

Blossom's gift is equally as meaningful—a woven Moses basket lined with soft muslin, a small hand-carved guardian angel nestled inside.

Alice waves the attached card. "This basket is for safekeeping, but not just for the baby. Tuck your worries here too. Let them rest when you need to breathe."

Even Janey has sent a gift: a stylish diaper bag packed with essentials. Her note reads, *Every new mama needs a head start. You've got this. And when you don't—text me.*

Alice unveils a game she's invented called Pin the Bottle on the Baby—her own baby shower twist on Pin the Tail on the Donkey. She's taped two oversized posters to the wall: one of a cherub-faced baby boy, the other of a rosy-cheeked little girl, both blissfully diaper-free. Across their round bellies, she's left space to write the names Sadie's been considering.

The plan is simple: Sadie gets blindfolded and handed a paper baby bottle. With everyone watching and cheering, she'll try to pin the bottle on the poster—and whichever name ends up closest to the bottle's tip will be the baby's "chosen" name.

But when Alice hands Sadie the marker and says, "Go ahead! Write down the names you've been thinking about," the room quiets.

Sadie stares at the blank posters. "I haven't picked any names," she says softly. "I haven't even thought about it, actually."

The mood shifts. Alice's smile falters. "Oh. Well . . . we can all help, if you want."

Sadie gives a small, weary nod, and for a moment, it's no longer just a game—it's a lifeline.

Taking the cap off the marker, Alice scribbles the names as we call them out. *Lila, Maisie, Emeline,* and *Bella*. She adds *Sadie Jr.* at the bottom, then scratches through it. "Just joking."

For the boys, she lists *Jude, Rowan, Hollis, Calvin,* and *Eli*.

At the sound of that last one, Sadie's head lifts ever so slightly. "Eli," she repeats quietly, as if trying it on in her mind. Something flickers across her face—surprise, maybe. Or recognition? Or is it pain?

Alice doesn't notice, already blindfolding her. "Okay, mama-to-be. Let's see where fate lands."

Sadie falters, momentarily thrown off balance by the blindfold, but Alice grabs her arm and gently steadies her. Together, they guide the bottle to the poster, and it lands squarely on *Emeline*.

A soft smile touches Sadie's lips when her second attempt hits *Eli* on the boy baby.

"*Emeline* and *Eli*," I say, grinning. "Perfect if you're having twins."

Sadie groans, her hand drifting instinctively to her belly. "I certainly hope not. I can't afford one baby, let alone two."

When the others migrate to the kitchen to start dinner, I stay behind in the living room to help Sadie organize her gifts.

"I think Eli is a lovely name for your baby—if it's a boy," I say, folding a towel and placing it on the growing pile of linens. "I get the impression there's an Eli in your past."

Sadie exhales sharply and drops into the chair behind her, a caterpillar rattle clutched in one hand. "Eli was my little brother. My parents struggled to have another child after me. They'd given up when seven years later, along came Eli—our surprise baby." She pauses, eyes fixed on the toy in her hand. "I'm from Florida. We lived on a lake on a golf course. One day, just after Eli's third birthday, he wandered too close to the lake, and an alligator got him."

I gasp, my hand flying to my mouth. "Oh, Sadie. That's heartbreaking. I'm so sorry."

Sadie nods, slowly. "My mom was sitting by the pool, reading a novel. She wasn't watching him. Thank goodness I was at school at the time. I don't think I could've handled seeing that. My parents were never the same afterward. They sold our house and moved to a subdivision—somewhere far away from any body of water." She strokes the caterpillar's fuzzy body with her thumb, her voice quieter now. "I love the idea of naming the baby Eli . . . but I don't know. Part of me feels like I'd be bringing him back. And part of me wonders if that's fair to either of them."

"I understand why you'd be conflicted. You'll know once you meet your baby." I lift my palms, a wry smile tugging at my lips. "Who knows? It might not even be a boy."

"True." A faint light returns to her eyes. "Secretly, I'm hoping for a girl." I haven't seen her eyes twinkle like that in days.

Standing, I offer her a hand. "Shall we go help the others with dinner?"

She takes it, allowing me to pull her to her feet. "If you don't mind, I'm going back to my room. I want to finish the assignment I'm working on."

I smile softly. "Don't overdo it, Sadie. Stress isn't good for the baby. If you deliver early, I'll give you plenty of time to complete your assignments."

She cradles the caterpillar like an infant. "I appreciate that, Selwyn. I'm just not myself right now, and I need to be alone."

"I understand. If you change your mind, you know where to find us. If not, I'll bring you a tray later."

In the kitchen, the party is in full swing. Blossom and Alice are mixing up a batch of margaritas, Griffin is patting out hamburgers, and Rosa is tossing a green salad.

Spotting me in the doorway, Griffin calls, "We're speeding up the process. Looks like a storm is heading our way. I've already started the grill."

Blossom hands me a margarita. "Happy birthday, Daisy."

"You knew?" I blink, surprised. But the truth is, I'd been secretly hoping someone would remember. I don't know why it matters so much this year. Maybe because both my parents are gone. Maybe because, for the first time in my life, I feel truly alone in the world. And somehow, this small act—someone remembering—makes me feel a little less invisible. A little less alone.

Blossom lowers her voice to a whisper. "You should know by now that you can't keep secrets from angels."

I laugh, taking a sip of the margarita. The salt on the rim stings just enough to pull me into the present. Blossom's words make me smile—but only on the outside. A part of me is upstairs with Sadie, curled around the ache she didn't quite say aloud.

I want to enjoy my birthday. I want to lean into the laughter, the clink of glasses, the smell of burgers on the grill. But it feels like I'm trying to dance with a stone in my shoe. She's just a girl, really. A girl about to become a mother, alone and unsure, cradling a stuffed caterpillar like it might whisper answers.

Blossom passes me a bowl of chips, and I force a brighter smile. I'm touched they planned a dinner in my honor. I'll talk to Sadie later. Maybe I can convince her to let me call her parents. She really needs her family right now. Having lost one child so early, wouldn't they cling to the one they still have? Instead, they've turned away.

Alice monopolizes the dinner conversation with a spirited analysis of Sadie's baby's zodiac sign. "If the baby comes early, it'll be a Gemini. Geminis are born to throw dinner parties and start podcasts. They're the baby whisperers of the zodiac—until they get bored and start a side hustle selling homemade granola."

"Hey! Easy. I'm a Gemini," I say, pretending to be offended. Though I fully admit I am easily bored.

"I am not dissing you, Selwyn," Alice says. "Geminis are the best—versatile, expressive, curious, and kind."

"All adjectives I'd use to describe Selwyn," Griffin says, smiling at me. "But what if Sadie goes to her due date? What zodiac sign will that be?"

"The baby will be a Cancer," Alice replies. "Cancers cry during commercials, but they'll also fight a bear to protect their family. If Sadie has a Cancer baby, that kid is gonna be the one everyone goes to for advice by the third grade."

Laughter erupts around the table.

As we're finishing dinner, Rosa quietly slips away from the table. A moment later, she returns, carrying a cake aglow with lit candles—her lemon buttermilk cake, soft and tangy, crowned with fresh berries—just like she used to make for me every year.

I blow out the candles, and as Rosa is slicing the cake, presents appear.

Rosa's gift takes my breath away—a Herend cross the yellow-green color of new spring growth, smooth and cool in my hand. Its unexpected beauty brings tears to my eyes.

"It's actually from your mama," she says, handing out plates of cake. "Miss Flossie bought it for you years ago, before she got sick. I guess she forgot to give it to you, because I found it in a drawer when we were cleaning out for the painters."

I clutch the cross to my chest. "It's beautiful. And so special. Thank you."

Blossom hands me a Simon Pearce crystal bud vase in the shape of a heart with a single blue hydrangea bloom—my favorite. "Because even the strongest women need a soft place to land when life gets heavy," she says with a wink.

Griffin's gift is a leather-bound photo album filled with pictures from our high school years. "When our days were simple and carefree," he says as I thumb through the pages, giggling at a few.

"Thank you, Griffin." I close the book, running my hand over the leather cover. "This is so meaningful. I can't wait to study every page."

"And from me," Alice says, plunking down a shirt box wrapped in glossy hot pink paper, a white, oversized pom-pom bow slightly askew on top—more exuberant than elegant, but unmistakably heartfelt.

"This is almost too pretty to open," I say, carefully removing the paper and lifting the lid on the box. Inside is what appears to be a manuscript. The title page reads: *A Portrait of Selwyn*.

Alice blushes. "I'm sorry. I used all your printer paper. I'll buy you some more."

My eyes narrow as I flip through the first few pages. "Is this about me?"

Alice shrugs, trying for casual, but there's a nervous energy in the way she folds her napkin into tighter and tighter squares. "Kind of. Just . . . observations. Things I've noticed. Stuff I made up too," she says, eyes fixed on the table. "You don't have to read it if you don't want to." There's something in her voice—like she's offering me a piece of herself and hoping I won't notice how fragile it is.

I trace the title with my fingertip, the weight of it pressing on my chest without knowing why. "You've been working on this for a while?"

She nods. "Off and on. I've been writing all my life. Nothing of any consequence—stories for children at first, then novellas for young adults. Just my imagination with the world I was missing out on. But this . . ." She gestures toward the boxed manuscript. "This I wanted to matter."

I look up and meet her eyes—those clear, searching eyes—and for a moment, something shifts in me. Not quite recognition. More like the echo of a memory I never made, or the tug of a thread I didn't know was there. Familiar, but just out of reach.

"Thank you, Alice. I can't wait to read it." I place the lid on the box. "This might be the most unexpected gift I've ever received."

Alice beams. "Well, you always say you're hard to shop for."

I laugh out loud. This child never ceases to amaze me. I don't recall ever saying that to her, but Flossie often accused me of being exactly that.

A flash of lightning illuminates the window, followed by a sharp crack of thunder.

I shrink back in my chair. "The storm is getting closer. Everyone who drove should think about heading out before it gets too bad."

"I think we're already too late," Griffin says, checking the weather app on his phone. "If you don't mind, I'll ride this one out here."

I peer over his shoulder at the radar. "That looks rough. Maybe you should stay too, Rosa. We have plenty of room."

Rosa pushes back from the table. "Sounds like a party. I wish I could, but I need to get home to my hubby." She heads to the laundry room for her things. "I hate to leave you with this mess," she adds, sweeping an arm toward the chaotic kitchen.

"No worries. The four of us will have this cleaned up in no time." When I open the door for her, the wind nearly rips it from my hand. I slam it shut again. "Are you sure about this?"

Rosa brushes past me. "I'm positive. I'll be fine. I'm not afraid of a little rain."

As she disappears into the stormy night, I call after her, "Text me when you get home!"

When I turn away from the door, Alice is clearing the table while Griffin and Blossom rinse dishes and load the dishwasher.

I'm drying the last pot when my phone rings, and Rosa's name lights up the screen. She hasn't been gone long enough to be home.

"There are trees down everywhere," she says, her voice

tight with panic. "If I weren't already halfway home, I'd turn around and come back. Just wanted you to know—it's bad out here. Griffin's better off staying put until it's over."

I meet Griffin's eyes across the kitchen. He's already watching me, concern etched on his face. "He's not going anywhere. Thanks for letting us know. Drive safely."

Ending the call, I look up at the three expectant faces. "Looks like we have a long night ahead."

Blossom covers a yawn with the back of her hand. "Then, I'm turning in. Nothing soothes the soul like the rain on the roof of my mobile home."

"You can't go out in this deluge," I say, glancing toward the window, where sheets of rain blur the view. "Give it a few minutes to pass. Let's find a movie while we wait."

"Yes! A movie!" Alice exclaims. "I'll take the gifts up to the nursery to get them out of the way." She's already darting across the hallway to the living room, loading her arms with packages before hurrying upstairs.

When she doesn't come right back, I assume she's checking on Sadie. Then her scream tears through the house. "Selwyn! Come quick! Sadie's having her baby—on the bathroom floor!"

Eighteen

Blossom, Griffin, and I race up the stairs to the hall bathroom.

Sadie is sprawled on the tile floor, her face slick with sweat, a smear of blood beneath her. Her legs are bent and spread, and she's screaming, "I need to push!" The words ricochet off the walls, raw and desperate.

"No! Don't push," Blossom says, alarmed.

"We need to get you to the hospital." I crouch to help her up, but she flails and strikes me across the nose. Pain explodes sharp and hot, and I taste the tang of blood as it runs from my nose.

She doesn't even notice.

"I can't make it to the hospital," she pants. "This baby is coming now."

Panic clamps down on my chest. I grab a towel and press it to my nose. "Call 911," I bark at Griffin.

"There's no time," Blossom says, calm and focused. "Griffin, Alice—clean towels and scissors. Go!"

She shuts the door behind them and heads to the sink, turning on the water and rolling up her sleeves.

"What're you doing?" I ask, stunned.

"Delivering a baby," she says, scrubbing her hands like a surgeon prepping for emergency surgery.

I gape at her. "Have you ever actually *done* this before?"

"Not exactly," she says, reaching for a hand towel. "But I know what to do. And right now, we don't have another choice."

"I'll get Janey on the phone—she can talk us through it," I say, my fingers trembling as I press her contact.

Sadie lets out a guttural cry as Janey picks up. "Selwyn? Is that you? Is everything okay?" Her voice, laced with concern, crackles over the speaker.

"Janey! Thank God I reached you! Sadie's baby's coming. There's no time to get her to the hospital. My friend Blossom is here with me. We need you to walk us through it. I'm putting you on speaker," I say, setting the phone on the floor.

Janey's voice steadies me instantly. "Hello, everyone. Let's all take a deep breath. I'm right here with you. And don't worry—this isn't the first baby I've delivered over the phone."

Sadie lets out another low moan as a contraction rolls through her. Blossom kneels beside her, dabbing gently at her brow with a cool washcloth. I press the towel tighter to my nose, blood still trickling.

Janey's soothing voice floats up from the floor. "Blossom, Selwyn—you've got this. Let's bring this baby into the world. Blossom—if you can, put a towel under her hips. Selwyn, you're the one she trusts. Let her see that in your face. Sadie, I need you to listen now—short, shallow breaths. Don't push unless we say."

Sadie moans, twisting onto her elbows. "I can't wait . . . I need to push . . . Now!"

"I know, honey," Blossom says, carefully adjusting the towel beneath her. "We've got you."

Alice cracks the door and passes in an armful of towels and a pair of scissors. "Can I come in?"

I take the items from her. "Not now, sweetheart. There's not enough room. But you can wait right here in case we need anything else. It shouldn't be long," I say, closing the door.

Janey's voice comes through again. "Sadie, with the next contraction, I want you to give a gentle push. Not all at once."

Sadie lets out a raw, primal sound and bears down. Blossom kneels between her legs, hands unwavering, eyes sharp with purpose. "The baby's coming," she murmurs. "I see the head."

I kneel beside Sadie, stroking her arm. "You're doing so well. You're not alone. We're right here."

With the next push, the baby slips into Blossom's hands— a small, slick body, limp and silent.

"It's a boy," Blossom says, her voice trembling ever so slightly.

But something's wrong.

"Oh, God," I whisper, a chill rushing through me. "Why isn't he crying?"

From the phone on the floor, Janey's voice breaks the eerie silence. "Give him a moment. Blossom, hold him face down and gently clear his mouth and nose with a clean towel."

Blossom follows her instructions, her expert hands moving with quiet precision as she pats the baby's back. "Come on, little one," she murmurs. "Let's hear you."

The silence stretches. One second. Two. Then, finally, a sharp, wet cry bursts from the tiny lungs, and we all exhale at once. The sound fills the room like music.

Blossom wraps the baby in a towel, then offers him to Sadie. But she turns her head away.

"No," she says, her voice hoarse and flat. "I don't want to hold him."

Blossom hesitates, her arms still outstretched. "Honey, it's okay. You're both safe now. He's here."

Sadie shakes her head, tears streaming down her face. "I can't. Please—I just can't."

Blossom, cradling the newborn, steps back, her expression unreadable.

I kneel beside Sadie, brushing a strand of damp hair from her cheek. "He's healthy, Sadie. You did something incredible."

"I don't feel incredible," she whispers.

I swallow hard, reminding myself how much she's just been through—body and soul. I glance at the phone, still on speaker. "What do we do now, Janey?"

"Nothing. Don't move. I'm outside. I'll be up in a minute." There's a click as the line goes dead.

Blossom places the baby in my arms, and I rock him gently, the hush of the room broken only by his tiny cries.

A moment later, there's a soft tap on the door, and Janey peeks in. When she sees the baby in my arms, her face lights up, and she enters the room. "Congratulations! You three did an excellent job."

"We couldn't have done it without you," I say.

"I'm glad I could help." Janey kneels beside Sadie, snapping on gloves and assessing her with practiced hands. "The baby's out. That's the hardest part. Once we deliver the placenta, we can get you off this cold tile."

Sadie moans, barely acknowledging her.

"You'll need to give me one more push," Janey coaches. "Just like before—only not as forceful this time."

Sadie groans but complies, summoning just enough strength for one last push. Within moments, Janey wraps the placenta in a towel and sets it aside.

"That's it. You did really well, Sadie." With efficient movements, Janey checks Sadie's bleeding, her expression focused but reassuring. "You're stable. Let's get you into bed. You've earned a nice, long rest."

I hand the baby to Blossom and open the door, motioning for Griffin to come in. Together, we lift Sadie off the floor and guide her slowly down the hall to her room. She doesn't say a word, her eyes fixed on some far-off point. Once she's settled under the covers, she turns away from us, facing the wall.

"She needs rest," Janey murmurs, and I nod.

We return to the bathroom where Blossom is still cradling the baby, humming low and sweet.

"Now, let's have a look at this little one," Janey says, taking him from her arms and laying him on a clean towel spread across the counter.

As she begins her exam, Alice slips into the room, her face pale but glowing. "Is he okay?" she whispers, her eyes locked on the baby.

"He's perfect," Janey says without looking up, her stethoscope pressed to his tiny chest.

Alice clasps her hands over her heart, her chin trembling as she fights back tears.

"He's small, but not too small. Probably about two weeks early," Janey continues, gently pressing his belly. "Good tone, good color. Strong cry. All excellent signs." She finally looks up at me. "He's healthy. No sense in making a hospital run tonight. The storm's passed, but I'd bet the emergency room is a madhouse. I'll have a pediatrician friend of mine stop by tomorrow for a full exam."

I exhale for what feels like the first time in hours. "That would be amazing. Thank you, Janey."

"He'll be hungry soon," she says. "If Sadie isn't up for trying tonight, don't hesitate to give him a bottle."

I gulp. Did we even buy bottles? Formula? I can't remember.

I walk Janey downstairs and hug her tightly at the door. "Thank you again—for everything."

"You're most welcome." She chuckles as she steps onto the porch. "That's one way to avoid hospital bills."

I laugh, a little breathless. "I hadn't thought of that."

Once she's gone, I tear through the kitchen—flinging open cabinets, checking drawers, rifling through bags. Nothing. Unless it's upstairs in the nursery, we don't have a single bottle.

"What're you looking for?" Griffin asks from the doorway, brows furrowed.

"Bottles. Formula." I slam a cabinet shut and turn to face him. "I don't think we have any."

He moves to the breakfast counter, scanning the chaos. "If you tell me what to buy, I can run to the store."

I shake my head. "I wouldn't even know where to start. There are like eighty different kinds."

Griffin fishes his keys out of his pocket. "Don't worry. I've got this. I used to keep a can of Similac and a clean bottle in the glove box."

I blink. "You did? Why?"

He shrugs, a small smile tugging at his mouth. "My youngest had reflux. I could mix a four-ounce bottle with one hand while lighting the grill with the other. It's a very specific kind of survival training."

Tension escapes my body and my shoulders sag. "You're the best, Griffin. Thanks."

"I'll be back in twenty," he says, already moving toward the door.

I head back upstairs to find Blossom perched on the edge of Sadie's bed, urging her to try nursing, while Alice hovers nearby, wringing her hands.

"Psst, Alice!" I call in a loud whisper, motioning her toward the door. When she joins me in the hallway, I lower my voice. "Did we buy any bottles or formula?"

Her eyes grow wide. "No. I—I forgot. I didn't even think about it. I'm so sorry."

"Don't worry, sweetheart," I say, giving her arm a reassuring squeeze. "Griffin's already gone to get some."

Blossom emerges from Sadie's room with the baby, closing the door behind her. "She's wiped out. We should let her sleep."

"She needs it." I reach for the baby, and Blossom transfers him into my arms. "Let's get a diaper on this one and dress him into proper clothing for his first meal."

We head into the nursery, and I lay him on the changing table. Alice doesn't leave my side, handing me everything I need without being asked—diaper, undershirt, soft cotton gown, tiny socks.

His body is so impossibly small, yet every part of him is whole. I run a finger along the curve of his cheek, over the downy fuzz at his temple. His eyes flutter closed again, content.

I pick him up, cradling him against my chest. And just like that, something inside of me changes. I can't name it, but I can feel it. I don't know what the future holds. I don't even know his name. But I'm already in love.

Downstairs in the kitchen, Griffin has returned from the store, set the coffeepot to brew, and mixed a bottle of formula.

"Even I got confused by all the options, and I'm a veteran." He holds up a package of Similac ready-to-feed bottles. "I figured I'd stick with what worked for my girls." He opens the package and hands me the bottle.

I glance from the bottle to the baby. "I've never actually done this. Maybe someone else should feed him the first time."

Blossom raises both hands. "I delivered that baby. I've done my part for the day. I'm going to bed. And you should too, Alice," she adds, already steering the girl toward the door.

I'm pretty sure she's giving me some time alone with Griffin, and I appreciate it. If I'm going to help Sadie, I need to learn everything I can about babies, and he clearly knows a lot more than I do.

"But I want to stay with the baby," Alice protests.

I offer her a sympathetic smile. "You'll have plenty of time with him, sweetheart. He's going to need you strong and steady in the days ahead."

Her face softens with realization. "I guess you're right." She jerks her hand away from Blossom but follows her out.

"Looks like you're it," I say, settling the baby into Griffin's outstretched arms. I hand him the bottle and a burp cloth, then pour two mugs of coffee and slide in the chair across from him.

I nod at my cup. "I hope this isn't decaf. I have a long night ahead of me. No way I'm sleeping with him on my watch."

"You two share the same birthday. That makes you kindred spirits," Griffin says, gazing down at the baby as he sucks on the bottle.

I smile. "I hadn't thought of that."

He adjusts the baby in the crook of his arm, the bottle angled just right. "So . . . is Sadie rejecting him? Most first-time mothers can't stand to be away from their babies, even for a minute. Second-time mothers are smart enough to let their newborns spend the night in the nursery so they can get some sleep."

I wouldn't know, I think. *I'll never be a first- or second-time mother.*

"I'm not sure what's going on with her, honestly. She won't feed him. Won't even hold him. I'm surprised. I thought that since she didn't have an . . ." My voice trails off, unable to say the word.

Griffin finishes my sentence. "An abortion?"

I nod, watching the baby's tiny fingers curl around the

edge of the blanket. "I thought she wanted to keep him. But maybe . . . maybe she just couldn't bring herself to end the pregnancy. That's not the same thing, is it? Everything's been so chaotic around here. I kept thinking we'd have time—to talk, to figure things out. To make a plan."

He tilts his head. "The best-laid plans, huh?"

I smile, thinking of all the things I'd planned to do with Sadie before the baby arrived. "Right."

We sit in silence for a while, the only sounds the soft gurgle of the bottle and the occasional crack of thunder in the distance.

After a while, he says, "Do you remember the night we broke into the pool at Coach Harmon's house?"

I choke on a sip of coffee, laughing. "We didn't break in. The gate was already open."

Griffin gives me a look. "It was his backyard. We were trespassing."

"It was July. It was hot. And we were seventeen and stupid," I counter.

"You cannonballed in, fully clothed. I thought you'd lost your mind."

"Really? Because if I remember correctly, you dove in right after me."

Griffin grins. "We should've been arrested. But you looked so damn proud of yourself—floating there like a rebel mermaid."

I laugh, shaking my head. "We got away with a lot back then."

His eyes linger on mine. "Not everything."

My fingers tighten around the coffee mug. I don't ask what he means. I already know. "No. Not everything."

I stare into the steam rising from my cup, thinking about all the plans we once made—the versions of ourselves we swore we'd become. Somewhere along the way, life got in the way. Choices, regrets, the quiet ache of roads not taken.

When the baby finishes his bottle, Griffin burps him, and we place him in the Moses basket in the living room. I urge Griffin to go home, but he insists on staying. "At least through the next feeding."

We stay up until the wee hours, trading stories about high school, our failed marriages, and the dreams we let go of somewhere along the way.

When the baby wakes again around three, it's my turn to give him his bottle. His eyes flutter open, then close again as he latches on. I watch his tiny fists curl against my chest and wonder if Sadie knows what a miracle she's made.

"See! Nothing to it," Griffin says, watching me burp him. "You'll be a pro in no time."

Time. I wonder how much of that I'll have with him—days, weeks, months. I already can't imagine my life without him. How will I survive when she takes him away?

"You need to get some sleep, Selwyn. Let's put him in his crib." He plucks a baby monitor from the pile of gifts. "We'll hook this up. Then you'll hear him if he stirs."

I carry the baby up the stairs and settle him into the crib while Griffin sets up the monitor.

"There. All set." He hands me the portable unit. "You get ready for bed. I can see myself out."

I kiss his cheek. "Thank you, Griffin. I don't know what I would've done if you hadn't been here."

"It was my pleasure. Glad to be of help."

After he leaves, I head down the hall to my room and crawl into bed fully clothed. But sleep won't come. Every creak and shifting shadow feels like a threat. Eventually, I give in—I return to the nursery, curl up on the daybed across from the crib, and drift off to the sound of his breathing.

Nineteen

I bolt upright from a deep sleep, momentarily disoriented until I remember where I am.

The nursery is aglow with the first rays of dawn, casting gold across the walls. Sadie stands beside the crib, staring down at her sleeping baby. She's dressed in sweats, her blonde hair still damp from the shower. Her eyes are red-rimmed, heavy with something deeper than exhaustion.

I rise from the daybed and move quietly to her side, unsure whether to speak. The silence between us stretches. "He's so peaceful," I say finally.

"Mm-hmm," she murmurs, eyes never leaving the crib.

I glance at her from the corner of my eye, searching for something—softness, awe, even fear. But her expression is unreadable.

"Did you get some rest?" I ask.

Sadie grips the crib's railing, her knuckles white. "Enough. I need to finish my assignments," she says, her voice flat and distant.

Class participation counts toward her final grade. I was prepared to waive it if the baby's arrival made attendance impossible. But standing here now, she looks remarkably well for someone who just gave birth—definitely on the road to recovery.

"You can still finish out the class, you know? Blossom and I will help with the baby."

Sadie nods slowly. "Thanks." She doesn't reach for him. Doesn't lean closer. Just folds her arms across her chest, like the only way to keep from breaking is to hold herself together.

I want to ask what she's thinking. I want to ask a thousand things. But I don't. Instead, I rest a hand lightly on her shoulder. "We'll figure this out, Sadie. One step at a time."

She doesn't respond, just keeps staring down at him, her arms wrapped tight around herself.

The baby stirs, blinking his eyes open. He stretches one arm upward, fingers curling in the air, then lets out a soft, sighing whimper.

I smile down at him, the ache in my chest tightening. "He'll want to eat soon. Would you like to try nursing him?"

Her lips press into a thin line. She doesn't look up at me. "No."

Her tone is not harsh. It's barely above a whisper. But it's final.

I nod, careful not to press. "Okay. I'll get his bottle."

She exhales slowly. "Thanks," she says with fear in her eyes, the silent storm she's trying not to let swallow her whole.

I leave Sadie standing by the crib and head downstairs, the baby monitor clutched in one hand. I move around the kitchen on autopilot—making coffee and readying the bottle —but my mind stays with Sadie and the baby. She won't touch him. Won't feed him. She's afraid, but not of him. This fear feels different. Like she's already letting go.

I shouldn't assume anything, but the distance she's placing between herself and the baby is undeniable. And the thing I can't admit—not even to myself—is how easily I'm already filling the space she's leaving behind.

When I return to the nursery with the bottle, Sadie is gone. Her bedroom door is closed, and the baby has gone back to sleep. Not knowing when I'll get another chance, I slip down the hall to my room for a quick shower and clean clothes. It feels strange to do something ordinary, something for myself—like I'm stepping back into a life I no longer fully recognize. In a few short hours, the baby monitor has become a permanent appendage, my third hand. I feel an almost primal need to know what he's doing at all times—whether he stirs, sighs, or simply breathes.

The baby is crying when I get out of the shower. I towel dry my hair, throw on yesterday's jeans, and hurry down the hall to the nursery. I savor these moments alone with him, unsure if today might be my last. My last hour. My last bottle. I assume Sadie will stay through the end of class, but she's so unpredictable lately. I have no way of knowing for sure.

After the feeding, we head downstairs to find Blossom and Griffin in the kitchen. Blossom is at the stove scrambling eggs, while Griffin unpacks baby items from a row of plastic Target bags stretched across the counter.

He smiles up at us as we enter the room. "Good morning. I made a Target run on the way over. Stocked up on some things you're going to need," he says, holding up a tube of diaper rash cream.

"That was really thoughtful, Griffin. Thank you. Did you get some sleep?"

"A couple of hours. I have an open house this afternoon, but I wanted to drop these off while I had the chance. How's the new mama this morning? Any better?"

I open my mouth to answer, but the doorbell rings—just as Alice bursts through the back door.

"Where's the baby? Can I hold him?" she asks, practically dancing on her toes.

"Sure. But let Griffin help you." I turn the baby over to him before going to answer the front door.

An attractive woman about my age stands on the porch, her black leather tote slung over one shoulder. "I'm Dr. Eva Blanchard with Willow Creek Pediatrics. Janey Sinclair asked me to stop by to check on a newborn."

"Of course! She mentioned you. I'm Selwyn Aldridge. So good of you to come." I step out of the way so she can enter. "The baby is in the kitchen. Would you like some coffee?" I ask over my shoulder as I lead her down the hallway.

"No, thank you. I've already had my caffeine limit for the day."

In the kitchen, I introduce her to the others. She gives them a polite but brief nod. "My young patients call me Dr. Eva. So, here's the little guy," she says, lifting the baby from Alice's arms.

Without ceremony, she lays him on the kitchen table, strips off his clothes, and begins her examination. We all watch in silence as she checks every inch of him, gentle but methodical.

When she's finished, she hands the half-dressed baby back to Alice. "He appears to be in perfect health. Are you the mother?"

Alice giggles, blushing. "No, ma'am. Sadie's his mama."

Dr. Eva nods. "I'd like to speak with her if possible. I'll need some information from her for the birth certificate."

I take the baby from Alice. "Run upstairs and ask Sadie to come down, please. Tell her the pediatrician is here."

"Yes, ma'am," Alice says, darting off.

She's back in a flash—before I've even finished redressing the baby. "She refuses to come," she says, breathless. "She says she's busy."

Dr. Eva raises an eyebrow. "Oh? Is that so?"

"Let's talk in private," I say, leaving Alice and Griffin with the baby as I lead her down the hall to my study.

I wait until we're seated to begin. "Sadie just graduated from the university. She doesn't have a job, and she's completely on her own. She seems to be struggling with motherhood—won't nurse, won't hold the baby. She hasn't said it outright, but I think she's considering adoption."

Dr. Eva nods slowly, absorbing this. "And the baby's father?"

I shake my head. "He refuses to take responsibility."

Her expression tightens. "What about her parents?"

"Unfortunately, her parents have cut her off. I'm her summer school professor. She's been staying with me while she finishes up her last few credits to graduate."

Dr. Eva's voice softens into the same calm reassurance I imagine she uses with anxious young patients. "She may feel like she needs their approval to keep the baby. Have you spoken to them?"

I press my thumb to the center of my chest. "Me? No. I hadn't even thought about reaching out. I guess I could try calling them."

"You have a reason now—to notify them of the baby." Dr. Eva hands me her business card. "If Sadie decides to proceed with an adoption, we can help her connect with a reputable agency." She rises to go. "Do you have plans for circumcision? It's optional, but if you'd like to schedule it, we can arrange that in the next few days."

"We'll get right on it," I say, walking with her to the front door. "Thank you for the house call, Dr. Eva. Sadie doesn't have insurance. Will you send me an invoice? Or I can pay the balance when we come for the circumcision."

She offers a smile that softens her features. "This one is on me. Kids get in trouble too often these days. I try to help whenever I can."

I think about all the students I've tried to help over the years—some receptive, others not so much. "That's good of you. In today's complicated world, they need all the help we can give them."

I've barely closed the door behind the pediatrician when Alice appears, thrusting a folded piece of paper at me. "What's this?"

"Sadie's mother's phone number."

I unfold the paper and scan the impeccable, tiny print—*Marilyn Harper*, followed by a number with an area code I don't recognize. "Alice," I say, leveling a look at her. "I warned you about eavesdropping."

She shrugs, completely unrepentant. "I wasn't eavesdropping. I was gathering intel. For the baby. Someone has to advocate for him."

Biting back a laugh, I wave the paper at her. "How did you get it?"

"I have my ways," she says with a sheepish grin.

I shake my head. "You should consider a career as a private investigator."

"Or a forensic accountant," she replies, dead serious.

I laugh out loud. "I think you'd be just perfect for the job. You never cease to amaze me, Alice Jones."

Inhaling a deep breath, I return my attention to the slip of paper in my hand. "No time like the present. Wish me luck."

I retreat to my study, close the door, and settle in at my desk. I stare at the slip of paper—the number belonging to the woman who turned her back on her daughter in her hour of need. The idea that anyone could do that to their own child sends a surge of anger through me. I punch the number into my phone and lift it to my ear.

It rings several times before she answers—her voice clipped and exasperated. "Yes?"

The words tumble from my mouth. "Mrs. Harper, my name is Selwyn Aldridge. I'm calling about your daughter." I quickly explain that I'm Sadie's summer school professor and that she's been staying with me since she got kicked out of the sorority house a week ago. "Let me be the first to congratulate you. You have a grandson, born late last night, two weeks early but perfectly healthy. Mother and son are doing just fine."

The line goes quiet for a beat, then: "Excuse me?"

I steady my voice. "You have a grandson, Mrs. Harper. Sadie gave birth last night. Two weeks early, but he's healthy. She's doing well physically, but emotionally, I'm concerned about her."

Another pause. Then, she snaps, "Why are you calling me?"

"Because Sadie won't. And because I think—no, I know—she needs support. Whether or not you believe she deserves it."

"She made her bed," Mrs. Harper says, her tone now hostile. "She knew the consequences of her actions."

I grip the phone tighter. *She made her bed?* What is wrong with this woman?

"She's a scared young woman, Mrs. Harper. Whatever *mistakes* she made, they don't justify you leaving her to figure this out alone. She needs her family right now."

Her silence crackles on the other end.

"I'm not asking you to fix everything," I continue, my voice thick with emotion. "I'm just asking if you'll come see her. Or at least call her. You might be the only person who can reach her right now."

There's a long, brittle silence. For a moment, I think I may have gotten through to her. Then—click. The dial tone hums in my ear like a slap.

I lower the phone slowly, my fingers trembling with

restrained fury. And heartbreak—not for me but for the girl upstairs, who's just been abandoned all over again. At least, Sadie doesn't have to know about it. I'll take that phone call to my grave.

The rest of the day passes in a kind of suspended quiet. Sadie never comes downstairs. We knock lightly on her door, asking if we can get anything for her. She responds with silence. Blossom even leaves a lunch tray in the hallway, but the food remains untouched.

Through it all, Alice stays with the baby. She rocks him, changes him, hums softly when he fusses. She refuses to let anyone else take a turn. "He likes me best," she says with a grin, but I know it's more than that.

By late afternoon, I finally settle in at my desk, trying to prepare next week's lectures. Across the room, Alice is curled up in the armchair, the baby asleep against her chest. She's become a natural with him. Fiercely protective with the kind of calm you can't teach. The only sounds in the office are the soft rhythm of his breathing and the quiet clack of my keyboard.

Then, out of the blue, Alice looks up, eyes bright. "His name is Sam."

I study the tiny face nestled against her shoulder. He stirs a little, one hand curling into a fist near his cheek. "Sam?"

She nods, completely certain. "I don't know how I know. I just do. He's a Sam. You know—like *Sam-I-Am*. From *Green Eggs and Ham*? He's persistent. Curious. Kinda bossy." She glances down at the baby. "He already gives off that vibe. Like, *I do not like this bottle, ma'am. I do not like it Sam-I-Am.*"

I laugh out loud. "Alice, you are something else."

Alice grins. "Then it's settled. He's Sam."

"I guess so. For now. Ultimately, it's Sadie's decision."

I turn back to my screen, but the name echoes in my head. *Sam.* It's not official. Not permanent. But for now—it fits.

Twenty

An hour later, I take the baby from Alice. "You've been holding him all afternoon. You're going to spoil him." I have no idea if this is true, but it sounds logical enough. "Go outside. Get some fresh air. Do your laundry. Something."

"I'll put away the rest of his gifts," she says, trailing me out of the room. "Then I'll organize a changing station down here, so we're not constantly running up to the nursery."

I smile back at her. "That's a great idea, actually. The laundry room would be the best place for that."

"I'm on it," Alice says, skipping ahead of me into the living room.

Blossom is preparing dinner when I enter the kitchen. "That looks delicious," I say, peering over her shoulder into the skillet. "What is it?"

"Shrimp and corn succotash. And I've got a pan of cornbread in the oven." She glances sideways at me. "I see you've got your hands full. Wanna feed him before we eat?"

I check the stove clock. "Sure. It's been four hours since his last bottle."

"And, of course, he needs a diaper change. He *always*

needs a diaper change." As if on cue, Alice appears in the doorway, her arms full of diapers, wipes, and a folding mat for the counter.

Once the changing station is set up in the laundry room, I change his diaper and fix his bottle.

Lowering myself onto a stool, I ask, "Should we call Sadie to dinner? Or take her a tray?"

Blossom doesn't look up from buttering chunks of corn bread. "Whatever you think best."

I glance down at the baby. "I offered for us to help take care of him while she finishes her class, but it's kind of presumptuous for her to assume we'd do everything, don't you think?"

Blossom doesn't answer right away. Just keeps buttering the cornbread like she's waiting for me to hear myself.

And I do. I sigh. "I know she just gave birth. I'm trying to be patient. I really am. But it's hard not knowing what she wants—or if she even wants him."

Blossom finally turns to face me, wiping her hands on a dish towel. "She's still bleeding, Selwyn. She woke up this morning in a body that doesn't feel like hers anymore. And now there's a baby crying in the next room that she's supposed to know how to love." She leans a hip against the counter. "Some girls fall in love with their babies the moment they see them. Others take a little longer to find their way. Doesn't mean they're bad mothers. Just means they're human." She lets that settle before adding, "You offered to help. And she's letting you. That doesn't make her selfish. We have to remember she's scared."

"She's not the only one," I murmur.

Blossom looks over, her eyes softening. "What're you thinking, Daisy?"

"What if she's already decided to give him up? What if this is her way of letting go?"

Blossom lowers herself to the stool beside me. "You've fallen in love with him. That's easy to see. And I don't blame you. He's an adorable baby, and he fills a void you've been carrying around for too long." She pauses, searching my face. "If Sadie decides to give him up, will you consider adopting him?"

I look down at the baby. "The thought crossed my mind," I admit softly. Then I shake my head, almost laughing at myself. "But it's ridiculous. I'm over forty. I'm single. What would I do with a baby?"

Blossom opens her mouth, but I cut her off before she can say anything reassuring.

"It's not happening," I say, more firmly this time. "He's not mine. And I will not let my emotions confuse the situation." I set the empty bottle down and stand. "Is dinner almost ready? I'm starving. I'll burp him while we eat."

Blossom chuckles. "Look at you, burping a baby and inhaling cornbread like a seasoned mama. You might not want the title, but you're already doing the job."

She rises slowly and returns to the stove before I can respond, leaving her words to settle like steam in the air.

Alice takes a dinner tray up to Sadie, leaving it outside her door. When I go upstairs later to get ready for bed, the food is still there, untouched.

I get up with the baby twice during the night to feed him. Sadie's door stays closed, and I don't see her again until the next morning.

Blossom and I are in the kitchen—I'm gulping down coffee while burping the baby, and she's folding a load of tiny clothes—when Sadie walks in. She looks awful. Same sweats from yesterday, her hair twisted into a messy bun. Pale. Hollow-eyed. I know she hasn't been eating, but from the looks of her, she hasn't been sleeping either.

She pours coffee into a to-go cup, murmurs, "I'll see you

in class," and slips out the back door without so much as a glance at the baby.

I jump to my feet, hurrying after her. "Sadie! Wait! We need to talk about the circumcision."

She stops on the walkway but doesn't turn around. "What about it?"

"If you want the baby to have one, we need to schedule it soon."

She lifts a hand and waves it dismissively. "Do whatever you think is best." Then she gets in her car and drives away.

Thirty minutes later, I arrive on campus to find Sadie seated at the back of the classroom—an abrupt change from her usual spot at the front. She doesn't join the discussion. Her hand doesn't shoot up to answer questions. She barely looks at me.

When class ends, I overhear another student ask, "You had your baby? Boy or girl?"

"Boy," Sadie replies before stalking off, head down.

My heart aches for her. The pain is written all over her. She shouldn't have to carry this alone. I need to talk to her— make her tell me what she's thinking. About her future. About the baby's.

But she doesn't come straight home from campus.

When an hour passes and she still hasn't returned, my worry morphs into full-blown panic. She has no money for gas. Or food. When's the last time she even ate? On Saturday? She skipped my birthday dinner. Did she touch anything at the shower? Where is she? Job hunting? Wandering? Lying unconscious with a head injury and amnesia?

Get a grip, Selwyn.

But the loop won't stop spinning. Did she get run over by a train? Hit by a bus? Is she meeting with an adoption service?

I'm in my study around four o'clock when I hear the front

door creak open. I rise from my desk and step into the hall, catching her as she's tiptoeing up the stairs.

I'd spent the past five hours rehearsing exactly what to say. But now that she's here—safe and alive—none of that seems to matter. Relief slams into me, followed closely by frustration. "Where have you been? I've been worried sick."

Sadie looks over her shoulder at me, but she doesn't turn around. "Walking around campus. You don't have to worry about me, Selwyn. I'm not going to hurt myself, if that's what you're thinking."

"That thought never crossed my mind, actually," I say honestly.

Sadie rolls her eyes. "Yeah, right." She continues up the stairs, leaving me with a fresh, gnawing worry—what if she *is* suicidal?

I don't see her again until class on Tuesday.

Afterward, I invite her to go for coffee. "We need to talk."

"Okay," she says, her voice low with resignation. "I need to talk to you about something too."

We walk the short distance to Starbucks. As we wait in line, I catch Sadie eyeing the breakfast sandwiches in the display case. I nudge her with my elbow. "Get one. You need to eat."

She places a hand on her soft belly. "I'm trying to lose this baby fat."

"You don't have much to lose. But skipping meals isn't the way to go. You need your strength."

"I guess you're right," she says, ordering a sausage, cheddar, and egg sandwich when we reach the counter.

We find a table on the patio outside and sit in silence for a few minutes—me sipping coffee while she devours her sandwich.

"I'm worried about you, Sadie. You're not the same young woman I met two weeks ago. That girl was determined to have her baby, come hell or high water. But you haven't even held him yet. I don't understand—what changed?"

She lowers her sandwich. "It's hard to explain. I thought I'd fall head over heels in love with my child. But when I look at him, all I feel is resentment. Resentment that he's ruining my life before it even started. Resentment that he's not a girl. That's awful to say, but I can't help how I feel."

Her gaze shifts to the courtyard behind me. "I'm not ready to be a parent, Selwyn. I thought I was, but I have no way of supporting him. And if I give up on my dreams, I'll end up waiting tables in a roadside diner, wondering what could've been." She spreads her arms wide at the campus. "Then what was the point? All my hard work for nothing."

I reach for her hand. "You should be proud of yourself, Sadie. You gave that baby life. That's not nothing. And giving him up? That's not the easy road—it's the selfless one. It's not selfish to admit you're not ready."

Sadie pulls her hand free, eyes flicking away. "I just want to finish this class and leave this town once and for all. Would you please reconsider the participation requirement?"

"On three conditions. Finish the week. Turn in all your assignments. And if you choose adoption, talk to someone who knows what they're doing. Get real guidance."

She steadies her gaze on me. "I was hoping you'd keep him."

The words find their mark—unexpected and heavier than I'm ready for. I open my mouth, but no sound comes out. Because the truth is, I'm not sure where I stand. Not about me —I've never wanted anything more in my life. But about her. What if a year from now she changes her mind and wants him back? I can't imagine the heartache of losing him. Then again . . . if she's determined to put him up for adoption, how could I stand by and let him go to a total stranger?

I choose my words carefully. "What you decide—whether

to raise him or give him up for adoption—has to be your decision. A clean one. One you can live with for the rest of your life. Because once he's gone, there's no getting him back."

She looks away again, and this time, I let her. I sit with the weight of her words and mine, feeling the enormity of what neither of us wants to say out loud.

I watch her walk away a few minutes later, her back straight but her shoulders heavy with everything she's carrying. And I stay there long after, wondering what kind of mother I would be—and whether life is offering me a second chance or simply asking me to be the bridge for someone else's.

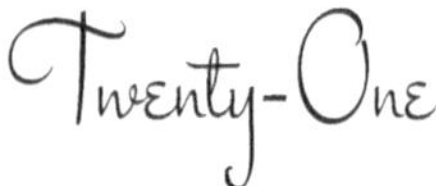

After our talk, Sadie seems a bit more pleasant, but her disinterest in the baby hasn't changed. I can't help wondering if she's already made up her mind about the adoption and is simply biding her time until class ends.

On Tuesday evening, I inform her of the baby's circumcision appointment at eleven the following morning. As politely as I can, I suggest she come along. I also mention that I'm covering the cost, hoping to avoid any awkwardness at checkout. She seems agreeable enough.

But after class on Wednesday, she disappears, and I don't see her again until I return home from the pediatrician's office. She's at the kitchen table, picking at a salad, when I walk in with the fussy baby still strapped into his infant car seat.

"Hey! Everything okay?" she asks, her voice neutral.

"His circumcision was today. Remember? I told you about it last night," I say, setting the car seat on the counter and unfastening the straps.

The color drains from her face. "Actually . . . no. I forgot. I'm sorry! Everything's been a blur lately."

I nod, swallowing my irritation. "I wish I could've missed

it too—poor little guy." I lift him gently from the seat, pressing a kiss to his warm forehead. "But he did great."

"Oh, good," she says, avoiding my eyes as she pushes a lettuce leaf around her plate.

"I need to get him changed. He's ready for a bottle," I add, already heading out of the kitchen.

Part of me expects her to follow, to offer to feed him, but I'm not surprised when she doesn't.

Later that afternoon, I'm in my study, working at my desk with the baby sleeping beside me in the Moses basket, when I hear the shower running upstairs. I assume it's Sadie—no one else is up there. Half an hour later, Sadie barrels down the stairs, shouting for Alice at the top of her lungs.

I step into the hall, finger pressed to my lips. "Shh! You'll wake the baby. What's going on?"

Alice emerges from the kitchen, wearing the expression of someone caught mid-crime. "Did you need me for something?" she asks, far too casually.

Sadie marches toward her, eyes blazing, waving her phone like a weapon. "I can't believe you did this. You've completely ruined my life."

"What did she do?" I ask, glancing between them.

"She posted *this* on my Instagram. She must have taken my phone while I was in the shower." Sadie thrusts the screen at me. "Look!"

It's a picture of the baby, bundled up and fast asleep. The caption reads: *Help me name my baby.*

I scroll through the comments. "Some of these names are actually quite clever."

Alice beams. "Right? There's even a *Sam!*"

I hand the phone back to Sadie. "But I can see why you're so upset."

Turning to Alice, I lower my voice. "You way overstepped this time. Taking Sadie's phone—violating her privacy—that's not okay. I simply can't have that in my house."

Alice's face crumples, her eyes shining. "I just . . . I thought maybe if her friends saw the baby—if they commented or congratulated her—it might make her feel proud. Happy, even. I wasn't trying to embarrass her. I just wanted her to see that people care. And they *do* care, Sadie. See?"

Sadie doesn't respond at first. She's still staring at her screen, her expression unreadable. Then something shifts. Her lips twitch, barely a smile.

"Jake just texted me," she murmurs. And without another word, she spins on her bare feet and bolts up the stairs.

Her bedroom door slams shut, leaving Alice and me in stunned silence.

The text from Jake sparks a sudden change in Sadie. After three days of keeping her distance, she can't seem to get enough of the baby. She handles him with ease—says she has years of babysitting experience. She changes him, feeds him, burps him. When he cries at night, though, I'm still the one who gets up.

Beneath it all, something feels hollow. There's a distance between them I can't quite name. She doesn't coo at him or linger in those quiet in-between moments. He squirms and cries in her arms but settles the moment I take him, like he knows who's been there for him all along.

My gut tells me her sudden enthusiasm has more to do with her phone than her son. She's constantly on her phone, texting Jake, I assume. And Alice, who follows her on Instagram, reports that Sadie is posting adorable baby photos and getting record-breaking likes.

The whole thing leaves me uneasy. Why is Jake suddenly

interested in Sadie and the baby? He ghosted her for months, denied paternity, wanted nothing to do with the situation. And now, out of the blue, he's sending flirty texts? Is it guilt? Boredom? Or something more manipulative? Maybe this is just about optics—because ever since Alice's little stunt on Instagram, Sadie's profile has blown up. Her followers are fawning over the baby like he's the next Gerber model.

From what I know about Jake, he's the kind of guy who likes attention—especially the kind that makes him look good.

I don't know what his motives are, but I don't trust the timing. Not when Sadie is vulnerable, grasping for any lifeline that might lead her out of this mess.

Worse, she seems dazzled by the attention. Hanging on every word he sends. Acting like the past never happened— like she didn't give birth alone on a bathroom floor with no one but Blossom and me there to catch the baby.

She's basking in it now. Smiling at her phone. Posting filtered pictures with hashtags like *#BabyBoyLove* and *#MyHeart*. But none of that changes the fact that she hasn't gotten up once in the night. When the baby cries, it's my arms he settles in.

Some part of me wants to believe she's just finding her footing. But another part can't help but wonder if Jake's interest—and maybe even hers—is more about how things *look* than how they *feel*.

Or maybe it's just the illusion of rescue—the fantasy that someone else will step in and fix everything. But fantasies don't change diapers at 3 a.m. Fantasies don't build a life.

And somewhere deep in my gut, a quiet voice whispers: *Be careful. This could all fall apart again.*

I express my concerns to Griffin when he stops by Thursday afternoon on his way home from work. We naturally gravitate to the swing—*our place*—where we won't be overheard by the *Wayward Wonders* inside the house.

He listens quietly while I express my concerns about Sadie and Jake. When I'm finished, he tilts his head, a knowing half smile tugging at his lips. "What are you not telling me, Selwyn?"

I blink. "What do you mean?"

"Don't forget who you're talking to." His voice softens. "I know you. I can see your soul."

His words strike a nerve—sharp, charged, and all too familiar. That was our thing in high school. A private phrase we whispered between kisses and shared secrets. *I can see your soul.*

I lower my gaze to my lap. "You don't know me like that anymore."

He lifts my chin. "You haven't changed that much. Come on, Selwyn. Talk to me. What's going on?"

I hesitate, finding the words. "In the beginning, Sadie wanted nothing to do with the baby. She wouldn't even hold him. I honestly thought she would put him up for adoption."

I swallow hard. "She even suggested I keep him. And I want to, Griffin. More than anything. I have this feeling—deep in my gut—that this baby is meant to be mine. But now everything has changed. Sam's father is back in the picture, and Sadie is suddenly happy again. Texting. Smiling. I have a sick feeling he's going to ask her to give him a chance. And she will. Which means she'll take Sam away." My voice breaks. "He's only a few days old, but I already love him so much. With my whole heart."

I don't even realize I'm crying until Griffin blots at my tears with a folded bandana.

"There now," he murmurs, wrapping his arms around me and pulling me close.

The feel of his body is so familiar it brings back the happier memories from our relationship. We were so good together once. I can't help but wonder . . . is it possible? Could we ever have that again?

But I push those thoughts away. I can't think about that now—not with everything else hanging in the balance. Not when a baby is asleep in the next room and a fragile girl is counting on me to help her figure out the rest of her life.

Later, maybe. When the dust settles. When I can tell the difference between comfort and something real. But not tonight. Tonight, I just let myself rest—tucked inside the warmth of what once was, without daring to hope too much for what might still be.

Eventually, my tears slow. I inhale a shaky breath and ease back from him. "I'm sorry. I haven't cried like that since . . . I don't know when. I didn't even cry at my mother's funeral."

"Then I'd say you were overdue." He leans back on the swing. "You know what the problem is, don't you?"

I shake my head. "What?"

"You have a big, beautiful heart with so much love to give. Have you ever considered adopting a child on your own?"

Only every day for the past six years, I think, but instead I say, "I'm too old. And single. No reputable agency will give a woman over forty a baby when there are younger married couples waiting in line."

"You're just barely over forty. And you don't have to be single, you know?"

I snort. "Ha. I don't see any eligible men beating down my door."

"You've been a little busy. Taking care of your parents didn't exactly leave time for dating. Maybe you should put the word out that you're available. Maybe try a dating app."

"That's not my style, Griffin. You know me better than that."

He nods. "Not mine either, actually."

I glance down at the blue bandana in my lap, damp with

my tears. "Besides, most men my age already have children from previous marriages. Nobody who is staring down the barrel of fifty wants to start over with a newborn."

He's quiet for a moment. "I would. I always wanted a third. I secretly hoped for a son. But Eleanor refused. Probably for the best. It would've just been another child for her to keep from me."

I study him quietly, unsure if I'm reading too much into his words—or if he's finally saying what I've been too afraid to admit I've wanted to hear. He's changed, but in the ways that matter most, he's the same. Reliable. Safe. Still able to read my soul when I've forgotten how to listen to it myself. And maybe that's what scares me. We couldn't make it work back then . . . but what if now is different?

Alice charges out the back door, stopping short when she sees Griffin. "Oh! Hey, Griff. I didn't know you were here." She turns to me, breathless. "Sam is screaming his head off, and Sadie is in her room on the phone. Can I give him a bottle?"

"Sure. Go ahead. I'll be right in."

Once she disappears, Griffin and I burst out laughing.

I nudge him with my elbow. "Since when does she call you Griff?"

He shakes his head with a playful grin. "That's a first. But I don't mind. I'm glad she feels comfortable giving me nick-names." Then, with a teasing glint in his eye, he adds, "Maybe adoption's not the best idea right now. You've already got your hands full with that one."

I laugh out loud. "Isn't that the truth?" Then I turn seri-ous. "She's actually really good with the baby, the perfect little mother's helper."

We stand, but neither of us moves to leave.

"I thought you said Sadie was taking responsibility for her

baby," Griffin says. "Doesn't sound like it to me if she's letting him scream his head off."

I shrug, a little exasperated. "She is—when it's convenient for her. I'm still the one getting up for middle-of-the-night feedings."

He frowns. "Don't let her jerk you around like that, Selwyn. Make her get up with him."

"Maybe I should," I say.

But the truth is, I cherish those quiet hours—the hush of the house, the warmth of his tiny body nestled against me, the way he gazes up at me like I'm his whole world. Something tells me I won't have this much longer.

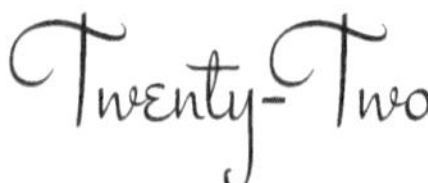

Sadie lingers after class on Friday, hovering near the door until the last of the students trickle out. When the room is empty, she approaches me, clutching her bag strap like a lifeline.

"Well," she says, voice a little shaky. "I guess this is it. I've turned in all my assignments. Does this mean I pass the class?"

"As long as your work holds up," I reply with a gentle smile. "Based on your past performance, I'm sure it does."

She blinks, then a grin breaks across her face. "So that's it? I'm officially a college graduate."

"You did it," I say. "Congratulations."

Before I can process what's happening, she throws her arms around me in a quick, tight hug. "You're the best, Selwyn. Thanks for everything."

Goose bumps rise on my arms. Something about her tone, her sudden burst of affection—it doesn't feel like a celebration. It feels like goodbye.

"Sadie—" I start, but she's already backing toward the door.

"I'll see you around," she says, too brightly, and then she's gone, bolting down the hallway before I can call her back.

Alarm bells clang in my head. I gather my things from my office in record time and make a beeline for the parking lot. I drive home fast, ignoring speed limits and rolling through stop signs, my heart pounding with every turn.

When I pull into the driveway and see her car is gone, the dread I've been trying to outrun slams straight into me.

I push through the back door, and Alice flies at me, sobbing. "He's gone! Sadie took Sam. Do something, Selwyn! Make her come back."

It feels like my heart is being torn from my chest, but I can't fall apart. Not when Alice already is.

I grip her shoulders. "Breathe. Just breathe. Tell me what happened."

She opens her mouth, but her words tumble out too fast, tangled and frantic.

I glance over her head at Blossom. "Maybe you'd better tell me."

Blossom's face is calm, but her emerald eyes brim with sorrow. "There's not much to tell. She flew in from class, ran upstairs, came back down with the baby, two suitcases, and his car seat. She'd clearly packed in advance."

"She didn't even say goodbye," Alice cries. "Wouldn't even let me hold Sam one last time. She snapped at me, told me his name wasn't *Sam*."

I exhale slowly. "I had a feeling something like this might happen." Pulling out my phone, I add, "After everything we did for her, the least she could do is offer an explanation."

I call her. Straight to voicemail. I try again. And again. Same result.

Finally, I type a message.

> This isn't like you, Sadie. I hope you know
> what you're doing. Please let us know
> you're safe when you get where you're
> going.

I set the phone down, my chest aching. "We need to try to see the bright side. Sam is Sadie's child, not ours. She and Jake want to make a family for him, and he deserves to have both his parents in his life. She wants a real career, and maybe now, with Jake involved, she'll have that chance."

Alice crosses her arms with a huff. "She was better off here. She had three extra parents helping her."

I wrap an arm around her in a half hug. "Yes, she did. And we did a good job. We helped her through an incredibly difficult time. That was our gift to her. In return, we got to love that sweet baby, if only for a short while. As the saying goes, *Better to have loved and lost than never to have loved at all.*"

Alice shakes her head. "I know you're trying to help, but it's not working." Her voice is flat. "I need to be alone right now." She slips out the back door without another glance.

I watch her cross the garden—shoulders slumped and head hung low—and traipse up the stairs to her apartment. "Poor kid," I murmur. "This is hard on all of us, but especially on her."

A sudden wave of weariness crashes over me, bone-deep and unshakable. "I think I'll go upstairs and lie down."

Blossom's arms close around me, solid and sure. "You do that. I'll be right here if you need me."

The chaos of the past week—Sam's sudden birth, the whirlwind of caring for a newborn, the quiet dread over Sadie's unraveling—catches up with me, and I fall into a deep, dreamless sleep.

I wake with a start, unsure of what time it is—whether it's still day or already night. My mouth is dry. My limbs feel heavy. The room is dim, bathed in soft orange light. Dusk. The silence is the stark reminder. No cries. No monitor buzzing. Just the distant hum of the air conditioner.

Downstairs, I find Alice curled up on the couch, her knees pulled to her chest, the crocheted throw clutched to her chin.

I sit down beside her, pinching her knee beneath the blanket. "Hey, kiddo."

"She'll come back, won't she?" Alice asks in a small voice. "I mean . . . she has to."

I hesitate. "I don't know, sweetheart. I wish I had answers. We'll just have to wait and see."

Alice sniffles, her voice cracking. "She didn't even say goodbye. She just left. Like none of it mattered. Like *he* didn't matter to us."

I stroke her wild curls. "You mattered to him. You loved him. He knew that. And don't you forget that."

The long weekend stretches out like an empty road. No class to teach. No baby to feed. No structure to hold the day together. Just hours—endless hours—of silence and space.

Alice stays in her apartment. She texts me once, letting me know she's fine, but I can see the lights are off. She doesn't come down for breakfast. Or lunch. I leave a plate on the back steps, but she doesn't touch it.

Blossom insists we all attend church on Sunday. Although I'd prefer to stay in bed, how could I say *no* to attending church with an angel? We walk home afterward, sunlight warming our faces, Alice trailing behind, pausing to peer into shop windows on the square.

I glance over at Blossom. "I was wrong—what I said to Alice on Friday. It isn't better to have loved and lost. It's much easier, *so* much easier, so much less painful, to never have loved at all."

She tilts her head toward me. "Come now, Daisy. What makes you say that?"

"It's true. I've lost every single person I ever truly cared about." My voice catches, but I keep on going. "Griffin was the first. He found someone better. Then my husband. He traded me in for a flawless model—one who could give him children. Both my parents, gone too soon. And now Sam." I pause, swallowing hard. "And Sadie. I loved her too."

Blossom walks beside me in silence for a few steps. Then, in that gentle voice of hers, she says, "You've lost people, yes. But that's not proof you shouldn't love. That's proof you can."

I glance over at her, uncertain.

She meets my gaze. "Heartache means your heart's still working. That you still have love to give. And one day— maybe sooner than you think—someone's going to need that love."

She lets that settle for a beat, then adds, "You're not done, Daisy. Not by a long shot."

Blossom's words stay with me throughout the day. *Heartache means your heart's still working. That you still have love to give. And one day—maybe sooner than you think—someone's going to need that love.*

Maybe so. But that doesn't mean I have to give it.

I need to stop handing out pieces of my heart to everyone who stumbles into my life. It's time I learn to hold something back. To protect what's left.

I'm in my study around five o'clock, grading Sadie's assignments, when there's a knock at the porch door.

Griffin stands there, hands in pocket, wearing a grim smile. "Can we talk for a minute?"

My stomach drops. *More bad news?*

I step outside and gesture toward the swing. "Want to sit?"

He glances at it, his expression flickering—nostalgia, maybe regret—and then shakes his head.

"I can only stay for a minute," he says, walking over to the railing, resting his hands there like he needs the support.

"I'm headed to Atlanta. Eleanor called last night." He lets out a hollow laugh. "She's talking about a reconciliation. Says she finally realized I wasn't such a bad husband after all."

I blink, stunned. This is the last thing I expected. "That's . . . great," I say, forcing a smile. "You can be a family again."

He turns to face me fully. "That's the only reason I'd even entertain the idea." His eyes find mine, searching. "But before I go, I need to know—would you ever consider giving me a second chance? Because my feelings for you never went away, Sel. And these past few weeks? They've only grown stronger." He steps closer, voice low and earnest. "We'd be good together. You know we would. We could start fresh. Adopt a child, even if it means going halfway around the world to find him. Or her. I don't care if it's a boy or a girl. I just want to spend the rest of my life watching you be a mother." Another step, and he's close enough to touch. "I chose the wrong woman back then. I see that now. But I don't want to make the same mistake twice. If you'll let me—I'd like to make it right."

I love him. I never stopped. But Eleanor will always have a hold on him. She'll use their daughters like pawns, and Griffin will bend—because that's who he is. A good father. A man who tries to make things right, even when the cost is high. Which means I'll always be the odd one out. That's heartache I don't need. This is my chance to walk away before I lose myself in it again. Before I forget that love alone isn't enough. That wanting someone doesn't make them mine. I've learned too much to go back now.

I take a breath. My chest aches, but my voice is steady. "I love you, Griffin."

His eyes flash—hope? Relief?

"But that doesn't change what I know."

He goes still.

"You're still married. You're still willing to entertain the idea of going back to a woman who spent years making you feel small. And maybe she's changed, or maybe she hasn't—but that's not my concern." I shake my head. "You need to make that decision for you, not for me. Not for some future you think we might have."

He swallows hard.

"I won't be part of anyone's almost," I say. "Not again."

He nods slowly. "I'm sorry."

"So am I," I whisper.

I don't wait for him to leave, don't watch his truck disappear from the driveway. I go back to my study, sit down at my computer, and reopen the grading portal.

Sadie's final papers are waiting there—neat file names, well-formatted, all turned in on time. Her last few essays aren't nearly as strong as her earlier work, and I grade them accordingly. I keep my promise. I don't penalize her for missed participation, for skipping out on the last week of class. But I give her a *C*—probably the only one she's ever earned. It won't hurt her GPA. She's already graduated. But it makes me feel better. A tiny, bitter triumph. Petty, maybe. But fair. She left without a word. Took the baby I love and disappeared like none of it mattered. She gets to move on. Fine, so do I. But she doesn't get an *A*.

I'm scrolling through my emails after class on Monday when I spot a subject line that makes me sit up straighter. **Urgent— Request for Meeting** from *Walter Gaines.*

Not only was Walter my father's closest friend, he's also the attorney who handled both my parents' estate matters. As an only child, I assumed the reading of my mother's will would be a formality—everything naturally passing to me. But *urgent* doesn't sound like a formality.

I shoot off a quick reply, letting him know I'm on my way home and will be there all afternoon. *Stop by anytime,* I write. *I'll be expecting you.*

He's waiting for me when I pull into the driveway.

He gives me a perfunctory kiss on the cheek. "Apologies for the abrupt request. A rather delicate matter has come up. We need to discuss it in person."

"Of course."

We head inside to the kitchen where Rosa is frying bacon for BLTs. When she sees Walter, the color drains from her face, and he gives her a curt nod. Their exchange strikes a chord.

Walter and Rosa have known each other for decades. They've always been friendly. What changed?

"Rosa, we'll be in my study. Please make sure we're not disturbed."

Rosa nods, her voice lowered. "Of course."

Walter pauses in the study's doorway—taking in the transformation from my father's dark, wood-paneled sanctum to a bright and airy room filled with light and life.

"I made a few changes. Dad is probably rolling over in his grave."

Walter smiles faintly. "I think Franklin would be pleased you're using his space. The fresh vibe suits you."

He roams the room a minute, pausing at the back window. I assume he's looking at the garden, but the intensity of his expression makes me wonder what he's really seeing.

"Shall we?" I gesture toward the love seat, settling into my comfy chair across from it.

He sits, crossing and recrossing his long legs. "I understand you have a young woman living in your garage apartment."

I narrow my eyes. "Yes. Alice. What concern is she of yours?"

"Several weeks ago, she left the group home where she's lived most of her life. The authorities have been looking for her."

My skin prickles, but I manage to keep a straight face. "Not very hard. She's been here for several weeks now."

"I understand. Officer Quinn reached out to the director at Waverly Hill after you discovered Alice in your garage apartment. That prompted her to reach out to me."

Waverly Hill. Alice's words echo in my mind. *I'm not allowed out at night at Waverly.*

"I don't understand. Why did they contact you? What do you have to do with Alice?"

He uncrosses his legs and leans forward, resting his elbows on his knees. "There's no easy way to say this. Alice is your half sister, Selwyn. Your father's daughter."

I stare at him in disbelief, certain I've misheard. "I'm sorry, what?"

"Your father had a relationship with one of his students years ago. Alice is the result."

"No." I shake my head slowly. "That's not possible. My father would've told me." But even as the words leave my mouth, I think of Flossie's note—the one with the funeral instructions. *Through thick or thin.* So, there *was* something going on with them. It happened right after I graduated from college, and I was wrapped up in launching my career. I never knew what it was about. I never bothered to ask questions.

"Your father thought it best for you not to know," Walter says gently. "Before his death, he had the court declare Alice legally incapable of making decisions about her health and well-being, and he appointed me her legal guardian. He worried about her future—constantly. His final wish was for her to remain at Waverly Hill, where he believed she'd be safe. From predators, from exploitation, from the world."

"From her sister," I deadpan.

Walter lets the comment pass. "I realize this is a shock."

"A shock?" My voice pitches upward as I jump to my feet. "I have a twenty-year-old half sister, and no one thought I deserved to know?"

Walter stands, too, hands raised in a calming gesture. "It wasn't my secret to tell, Selwyn."

I step back. "But it was yours to keep. My father's been dead for three years. Were you *ever* going to tell me?"

He shakes his head. "Your father insisted you never find out. He didn't want you burdened with his mistake—his illegitimate child."

Questions swarm my mind like bees on a hive. "Did Flossie know about Alice?"

Walter grimaces. "I was afraid you'd ask that. Yes, Flossie knew. She was furious when she found out about Franklin's affair. She would've left him, if not for the public humiliation of divorce. Alice was around five when her mother left. Your—"

My hand shoots out. "Wait! Stop! What happened to Alice's mother?"

"She took off in the middle of the night. Left Alice in their apartment alone. She called Franklin the next morning to tell him she wasn't coming back. She hasn't been seen or heard from since."

I sink back into my chair, the wind knocked clean out of me. "She left her? A five-year-old? Alone?"

Walter nods solemnly.

My chest tightens. "And my father just . . . locked her away at Waverly? Hid her like a secret shame?"

"Not at first," Walter says. "Franklin begged Flossie to let him bring Alice here. He desperately wanted her with him, to raise her, to introduce her to you. But your mother refused."

I grunt. "I'm not surprised. How would Flossie have explained Alice to her friends?"

"That's only part of it. She was also worried about taking care of Alice with her . . . challenges."

"Right. Because Alice is flawed. And Flossie only accepted perfection."

I bury my face in my hands, trying to grasp this revelation. Despite my best efforts, I was a disappointment to my mother. She never said it outright, but she constantly compared me to other girls—the stylish, pretty ones who married well and gave their mothers grandchildren.

The image of Alice flashes through my mind—her sweetness, her eagerness to connect, the way she clings to those she trusts. No wonder she watches from the shadows. No wonder she's afraid to speak up. Everyone who was supposed to love her either left or lied.

I drag my hands down my face. "How long has Alice known about me?" I ask, afraid to look up at him for fear of what I might find on his face. In his eyes. More truths. More pain.

"From the beginning." Walter's expression twists, as though the words cost him something. "Franklin didn't keep secrets from her. Keeping her at Waverly broke his heart, even though he believed it was for the best."

"How did she get here?" I ask, toying with a paper clip between my fingers.

"I don't know for sure. But if I had to guess, I'd say Rosa brought her here."

My head snaps up. "Rosa? She was in on this too?"

"That shouldn't surprise you, Selwyn. Your father and Rosa were very close."

I drop my gaze again. As I unbend the paper clip, I think about all the mornings I found the two of them at the kitchen table, heads bent over coffee, speaking in hushed tones. Were they whispering about Alice all along?

I swallow hard. "What now?"

"Alice will return to Waverly. Where she belongs."

Sensing movement outside, I glance past Walter toward the window. Across the garden, Officer Quinn and a woman in plainclothes are dragging a screaming Alice down the apartment stairs.

I leap to my feet and tear out the door, racing across the lawn to meet Blossom and Rosa in the driveway.

Alice's cries pierce the air, raw and frantic. "Please! Rosa! Save me! Don't let them take me back there!"

Before I can reach her, the patrol car door slams shut. The siren stays silent, but the engine hums with finality as they drive away.

Her tear-streaked face appears in the back window, eyes wide with terror, hands pressed to the glass. The image sears itself into my heart.

Rage ignites in my chest. I spin on Rosa. "How dare you betray me?"

Tears well in her eyes, but her voice doesn't waver. "I didn't betray you, Selwyn. I honored your father's wishes. My hands were tied. But your mother's death changed everything. I was trying to make it right—for both you and Alice."

I shake my head and clamp my hands over my ears. "I don't want to hear your excuses. Get your things and leave my house."

Rosa opens her mouth to speak, then thinks better of it. She brushes past me on her way inside, her silence louder than words.

As she walks away, I catch sight of Walter slinking toward his car. But I let him go. *Coward.*

Blossom takes a cautious step toward me, her face soft with concern.

I shake my head before she can speak. "Don't."

Turning away, I retreat to my study, the weight of it all pressing down like a storm cloud. I close the door behind me, shutting her out—shutting everything out.

The leather groans beneath me, familiar and worn, like the weight of everything I've just learned. My gaze lands on the corner of the old photograph peeking out from beneath the blotter. I slide it free with trembling fingers. *Alice.* The little girl with chubby cheeks and a halo of white-blonde curls was my father's other daughter. My half sister.

My chest tightens. All this time, she was here—hidden in

plain sight. And now, everything I thought I knew has changed.

I'm back on my feet. My skin feels too tight, my breath too shallow. I pace in slow, useless circles around the room, overwhelmed with sadness but too furious to cry. I don't know who I'm upset with the most.

I'm disappointed in my father for having an affair. But Flossie is the one who forced him to keep Alice hidden away. She stripped him of the chance to raise his daughter, to give Alice a proper family. To give me a half sister. Why? Was it revenge for cheating on her? Or was it really her fear of bringing imperfection into her perfect home?

And Rosa? I want to scream at her, but deep down I know —she was just being loyal. Loyal to a man she respected. Loyal to me, in her own twisted way.

The truth is, I don't know where to put all this pain. Every time I try to land on blame, it slips out from under me.

Everyone knew about Alice except me. I don't get it. "Why did they deprive me of the opportunity to know my half sister?"

I don't realize I've said it aloud until Blossom answers me from the doorway. "Isn't it obvious?"

"Obviously not." I zero in on her face, unable to read her expression. "I'm not in the mood for mind games, Blossom. What are you thinking?"

"It's simple, really. They didn't tell you about Alice because they knew you'd insist on bringing her here to live with your family."

Her words knock the breath from my chest. Because it's true. I would have fought for Alice. I would've loved her, even when I didn't understand her. Even when no one else could. But I was never given the chance.

"So, they deprived me of the opportunity to know my sister—and her, me. We missed out on twenty years of sharing each other's lives. And now they're dead, and I can't even tell them how angry I am about it."

The silence that follows is deafening, and for the first time in my life, I don't know who I'm grieving more—my parents, or the version of me that believed they always had my best interests at heart.

Twenty-Four

I sink into my favorite chair, but the soft down cushions offer little comfort. The room is too quiet. The house feels too big, like it's holding its breath. Every sound—every creak, every tick of the clock—only reminds me no one else is here. They're all gone. Dad. Flossie. Sadie. Sam. Alice. Griffin. Rosa. And for the first time, I let myself feel it fully.

I press my palms against my eyes, letting the anger turn to ache. There's no one left to blame, but I can't seem to stop trying. I don't even realize I've started to rock myself until my breath hitches. I bite down hard, holding it all in, but it rises anyway. A sob, raw and sudden, breaks through my throat. I cry myself to sleep, and when I wake on the sofa an hour later, the ache in my chest returns immediately, like a bruise being pressed. I swing my legs over the edge and rise slowly on shaky legs.

I wander through the empty rooms like I'm underwater— lungs tight, drowning, everything muffled and far away. The house feels too still. No baby crying. No Alice's delighted giggles. No bottles to warm or diapers to change. No Alice peppering me with endless questions about everything. Only the faint hum of the air conditioner and the ticking of the old clock on the living room shelf.

I find myself standing in the nursery doorway, staring, unable to step inside, unable to walk away. The crib, empty. The rocking chair, still. Rosa's quilt draped across the crib's railing. He was never mine. I know that. But love doesn't care what's legal or logical. It only knows what it misses.

But Alice *is* mine. *My* half sister. *My* family. And we were robbed of each other.

Late afternoon, I find myself in the kitchen, watching the kettle whistle steam into the air, its shrill cry distant and unreal. I don't move—don't reach for a mug or pour water over the tea bag. I'm frozen—adrift in the thick fog of everything that's happened—when a face suddenly appears at the back door window. The young man looks vaguely familiar, but my mind is slow to catch up. It's only when I open the door that recognition clicks into place. The guy from the medical equipment company.

He lifts a hand, wiggling his fingers. "Hello, ma'am. Remember me? I'm Jack Brunson."

I look past him at the pickup idling in the driveway. A magnet bearing his logo is fixed to the driver's door. *Jack of All Trades.* "I remember."

He grins. "Great. Nice to see you again. I was in the neighborhood and thought I'd stop by. Are you ready to get rid of your mildewed sofa? I'm free this afternoon. I can take it— and anything else you'd like—to the dump."

I think of the boxes of Flossie's belongings stacked in the garage. Her neatly folded clothes. Her matching handbags and pressed linen napkins. Suddenly, I can't get rid of them fast enough.

I want no reminder of the woman who cost me so much, who deliberately kept my sister from me.

"Your timing is impeccable. I may be able to fill up your truck three times over."

I turn off the kettle and follow him outside. His helper climbs from the passenger side, and together they wrestle the sofa and chair out of the garage and into the bed of the truck. I feel no remorse—no anything, only emptiness—as they haul away Flossie's boxes. How different my life might have been if she'd been more accepting of others. More real, less rehearsed. More focused on the love of family than putting on a flawless show for the outside world.

I don't realize Jack is speaking to me until he waves a hand in front of my face. "Hello. Are you okay?"

I shake my head, clearing the cobwebs. "Yes. Sorry. I'm preoccupied with other matters today."

"I understand. Is there anything else you want us to take? The truck's full now, but we can come back for a second load." He glances toward the garage apartment. "Is that an attic? Anything up there you want to get rid of?"

I consider his question. Aside from the brief moments when we discovered Alice, I haven't been in the apartment in years. "I'm not sure. But whatever is up there, I'll need to go through it first. I have your number, Jack. I'll call you when I'm ready."

"Fair enough." He tells me how much I owe him, and I go inside for my wallet.

After Jack leaves, I climb the steps to the apartment, wondering if Alice left anything behind. Officer Quinn and the Waverly woman hauled her out of here so quickly—did they even give her a chance to pack her things?

The one-bedroom apartment isn't up to Flossie's standards of interior design, but it's comfortable enough with modest furniture and a small kitchenette. I check the closets and look under the bed, but I don't find a trace of Alice.

I plop down on the sofa, needing a minute to collect my

thoughts. The pair of living room windows offer a clear view of the back of the house. From here, Alice could see straight into my bedroom and my study. The idea doesn't creep me out anymore—now that I know she's my sister, not just another misfit at the Porchlight Inn.

Glancing down, I spot a stack of envelopes wedged between two sofa cushions. I tug them free—a bundle tied with a blue gingham ribbon. The sight of my father's handwriting sends a jolt through me. He used to write often when I was away at summer camp, and later, during my college years at Washington and Lee.

I shouldn't invade Alice's privacy, but I can't help myself. I untie the ribbon and open the first letter.

They're filled with updates—his lectures and students, Flossie's garden parties, my milestones at school. He writes about me with pride, about Flossie with caution, and about Alice with unmistakable tenderness.

Each letter feels like a lifeline, his attempt to tether her to a world he couldn't share. But the more I read, the more I wonder if his carefully penned words only deepened her isolation. A window isn't the same as a welcome.

He talked about his wife. His daughter—me, not Alice. How must it have felt to read about a life she was never invited into? To know her father loved her, yet kept her hidden, always at a distance? He didn't mean to be cruel. But even love, when hidden, can feel like abandonment.

For the first time, I begin to grasp the weight Alice has carried all these years—her silence, her longing, the way she watched from the shadows. And I want to know more. About her life at Waverly. What it felt like to live in the shadows, kept out of sight.

Then I remember the novel she gave me for my birthday— the one she *wrote* for me—and I rush back through the garden to my study. I stretch out on the sofa, the box of pages resting on my stomach, and begin to read. I only pause for bathroom breaks and to fix a pimento cheese sandwich for dinner, then dive right back in. I read straight through to the end, finishing sometime after midnight.

The story is an adult fairytale about a young woman—a peasant—who watches from afar as her half sister reigns as the royal princess. She sees the grand dresses, the castle walls, the way the people cheer for someone who doesn't even know they exist. But instead of resentment, the peasant girl feels wonder. Curiosity. Longing.

The prose is lyrical—her descriptions read like poetry—and the story is quietly heartbreaking in its sweetness. There's magic, yes, but it's the ache beneath the magic that undoes me.

And then it hits me: Alice may have been at my wedding. She might have watched from the shadows as I glided down the aisle on our father's arm, wrapped in yards of creamy satin. I was the one with the elaborate flowers, the string quartet, the carefully chosen vows. Not her.

And Alice—my half sister—wrote me a fairytale instead of a toast.

When I finally turn the last page, I realize my cheeks are wet with tears. Her words have cracked something open in me, something soft and fragile I hadn't touched in years.

Later, as I'm getting ready for bed, I notice a light on in the garage apartment window. Did I leave that on—or did Alice?

It casts a soft, steady glow across the yard, cutting through the shadows like it has no intention of fading.

I stand there a moment, watching it. Maybe it's just a forgotten light. Or maybe it's something more. A sign. A reminder. A promise that where light lingers, love can still take root.

I don't know what tomorrow holds. But I know this: I'm not ready to let Alice go.

I oversleep on Tuesday morning, and for the first time ever, I call in sick for work.

When I go downstairs for coffee, Blossom is at the stove, poaching an egg. She flashes a bright smile at me. "Feeling better today?"

I pull a mug from the cabinet and slam the door. "I didn't think it was possible, but I actually feel worse. My heart literally aches in my chest." I fix my coffee and sit down at the counter. "I'm taking the day off work."

"Good for you. Everyone needs a mental health day every now and then." Blossom lifts the egg from the pan and eases it onto a slice of buttered toast. She adds two sausage links to the plate and sets it in front of me.

"Thanks, but I'm not really hungry," I say, pushing the plate aside.

Blossom sits down beside me with a cup of tea. "I left you alone last night. I figured you needed some space. Did you get any dinner?"

"I fixed a sandwich." I take a tentative sip of coffee, trying to steady myself. "And I read the novel Alice wrote about me. I was so engrossed, I couldn't put it down. I read straight through to the end. Her prose is beautiful—lyrical, really—and the story . . ." I pause, swallowing the lump in my throat. "It's touching in a quiet, aching sort of way. Bittersweet. She's incredibly talented. And the way she captured everything—what it must have felt like to watch from the outside, to want to be part of something without ever being invited in—it broke me a little. It's not just a story. It's her heart on paper."

Blossom dunks her tea bag several times before removing it from her mug. "She didn't just write you a story, Selwyn. She gave you her truth—wrapped in wonder and woven with hope. That's not something people do unless they love you deeply." She places her hand over mine. "You saw her. You see her. And now, thanks to that story, you're starting to feel what she's carried all along. That kind of connection"—her voice softens—"doesn't go away overnight. It's the beginning of something, not the end."

I pull my hand back gently, wrapping both palms around my coffee cup like it might anchor me. "My father thought it best for her to stay at Waverly," I say, more defensively than I mean to. "He believed that was the safest place. He had his reasons." The words sound hollow, even to me.

I shake my head, staring into the swirl of cream in my mug. "It's not that I don't care. I do. But I'm not ready to make any big decisions, Blossom. I need time to think. To breathe. Everything's still too . . . raw."

Blossom nods, though I can't quite tell if she understands or if she thinks I'm making a mistake. "So, what now?"

"I'm not sure. I may go back to bed. I may stay there for the rest of my life," I say, propping my elbows on the counter.

Blossom clicks her tongue. "So, you're gonna wallow?"

I've never been one to wallow in self-pity, but that's exactly what I feel like doing. "Pretty much, yeah."

"Your problems won't sort themselves, Daisy."

I let her words hang there—heavy and unwanted. I don't respond. I'm too tired to argue. Too emotionally strung out to care. I lay my cheek flat against the cool surface of the counter and close my eyes.

I've been stripped of everything—my illusions, my certainty, the carefully built walls I thought were protecting me. All gone. What's left is this brittle shell of a life I no longer recognize.

With my eyes still shut, I focus on the hum of the refrigerator—the only thing in this house that hasn't lied to me, left me, or let me down. It's the one steady sound in a world that's come completely undone.

I hear Blossom moving quietly around the kitchen, the soft clink of a mug, the shuffle of her slippers against the floor, the faint squeak of a cabinet door. She doesn't say a word, just moves with the kind of grace that comes from knowing not to fill silence with noise. I'm grateful she doesn't press me, doesn't try to fix it or make me talk. Her presence is enough—silent and solid and steady, like the hum of the fridge.

Eventually, I drag myself upstairs. I don't shower. I don't change. I crawl back into bed fully dressed, curling around a pillow like a child. I tell myself I'll just lie here for a few minutes. I stay for hours.

The rest of the day passes in a fog. I binge watch a series I've already seen, just to keep the thoughts at bay. But they come anyway. The guilt. The regret. The ache that spreads through my chest like the tide slipping out to sea—slow, silent, and impossible to stop.

I should've known. I should've seen. I should've asked more questions.

I think of Alice's face when they dragged her down the steps. How her voice cracked when she called out for Rosa. How she didn't call out for me. And why would she? I did nothing to stop them.

The more I think about Alice's story, the more I'm convinced there's something I overlooked. Late that afternoon, I tiptoe down to my study, quiet, so Blossom—who is banging around in the kitchen—doesn't hear me. I grab the novel and hurry back up to my room.

I lie in bed with the box of pages beside me. I warn myself not to read it again, that it will only hurt more the second time. But I flip it open anyway. This time, I don't skim. I read slowly. Carefully. Line by line.

The peasant girl doesn't just watch from afar—she waits. Hides behind stone pillars. Slips secret notes into hollow trees. Dreams of sitting at the royal table, not for power but for belonging.

I don't want your crown. I just want to know if we'd laugh at the same things.

She writes letters in the dirt with her fingertip. Wears bright colors to stand out from the other peasants. But the princess never sees her. Until one day, she does. A flicker in the crowd. A shadow in the garden. For a moment, their eyes meet.

She didn't wave. She didn't smile. But she looked at me. And that was everything.

At the end, the peasant girl vanishes into thin air. Not because of magic, but because she believes she doesn't belong in the story after all.

Some girls are born into the story. Others vanish quietly between the lines.

I stare at the last page, a sick twist forming in my gut. Alice wrote herself out. Did she know? Did she somehow sense that her time here was limited? That someone would come to drag her back to that place? Did she write this as a warning—or a goodbye?

If she ever reads this, I hope she knows—just for a moment, I believed I belonged."

The ache in my chest sharpens. *She believed she belonged.* Past tense. She left me this story not to impress me. Not even to flatter me. She left it as a lifeline. And I didn't reach for it in time.

I press the thick sheaf of pages to my chest and roll to my side, curling around them like a child clutching a favorite blanket. I have no idea how to make this right.

Twenty-Six

Something shifts inside me during the night—not loud, not dramatic. Just a quiet certainty: I can't let Alice be lost to me. Not again. Not like this. I find Blossom in the kitchen, and the words tumble out before I even sit down.

"What do I do, Blossom? How do I make this right?"

"You could start by talking to Rosa," Blossom says without hesitation, as though she's given it plenty of thought. "She knows every side of the story, and she'll give you an unbiased perspective."

"Will she even talk to me? I was pretty rude to her the other day."

Blossom hands me a steaming mug of coffee. "Of course she'll talk to you. She understands you were upset. She loves you, Daisy. She's been with your family since you were a wee child."

"But she worked for my parents, not me."

"She works for you now. And what's the difference? Her loyalty's always been to your family." She dunks her tea bag in her mug several times before tossing it in the trash can. "So, what's the plan? You springing Alice from that dreadful place?"

"How do you know it's dreadful? Have you been there?" My hand shoots out. "Never mind. Don't answer that. Of course you know."

I blow on my coffee. "I don't want to leave her there, but what other option do I have?"

"Do you really have to ask?" She sweeps an arm around the room. "You've got this big, beautiful home—your family's home. And she's your family. Why not open it to her?" She lets the words hang before adding, softer this time, "You've both lost your parents, but you still have each other. That poor girl has been wronged all her life. You have the chance to make something right."

I chew on my lower lip. "But what about her challenges? I've never been a parent. I know nothing about raising a girl with special needs."

Blossom lifts an eyebrow. "Raise her? She's a twenty-year-old young woman. She doesn't need parenting. She needs a place to land. Someone to help her find her footing in the world." She tugs her cardigan tighter around her shoulders. "As for her challenges . . . she lacks certain social filters, sure, but that's not a flaw. It's part of her charm. She doesn't offend people. She delights them. She might be a little pushy, but only when she's trying to get us to do the right thing. But you already know all this."

My eyes drift to the window. The light is still on in the garage apartment. A small thing, but somehow it feels like she's still here. Like she's waiting.

I feel Blossom's eyes on me, studying me. "What's really holding you back, Daisy?"

I look her straight in the eye and admit the truth. "Alice is another person for me to get attached to—only to leave when she no longer needs me."

Blossom leans into me, shoulder to shoulder. "Stop feeling sorry for yourself, Daisy. Maybe this time, someone's going to stay."

"I just don't get it, Blossom. It was so out of character for my father to have an affair. But even more so for him to keep his child locked away like a prisoner."

Blossom sets down her mug. "He wasn't trying to be cruel, Daisy. He was trying to save his marriage. Protect his image. Maybe even protect you. People do out-of-character things when they're desperate to keep the life they've built from falling apart." She pauses, eyes softening. "Doesn't make it right. But it does make it human. In his own way, he thought he was doing what was best—for everyone."

"According to Walter, Dad never wanted me to find out. He didn't want me burdened with his mistake—his illegitimate child." I stare down at my coffee, turning Walter's words over in my mind. "Alice is not a mistake. And she's not a burden."

"No, she most definitely is not."

I think about her novel. The way she looked at me, wide-eyed and hopeful, like she'd waited her whole life for me to see her. And I let her down. So did everyone else. But I still have time to do something about it.

I reach for my phone and send Rosa a text before I change my mind.

We need to talk.

She responds right away.

Meet me at Bottletree in thirty minutes. I can't come to the house. I'll explain when I see you.

Bottletree Bakery is Oxford's go-to spot for fresh pastries and a good strong coffee—equal parts bakery, coffee shop, and front porch for the town's morning crowd. When I arrive, Rosa is already seated at a table in the back, a lemon cream cheese and blueberry Danish waiting for me—my favorite. A pang of guilt tightens my chest. She knows me better than my own mother ever did. And I was so awful to her the other day. *Get your things and leave my house.*

I pull her to her feet and into my arms. "I'm sorry about the things I said. I was wrong to accuse you of betraying me."

She strokes my hair, a gesture so achingly familiar it brings tears to my eyes. "I understand. You were in shock."

We sit down across from each other. I pinch off a bite of Danish, but my hands stall halfway. My stomach is too knotted up to eat.

"Thank you for meeting me here. Your parents were both so good to me, I wouldn't feel right speaking ill of them in their own home," she explains.

"I understand why you'd feel that way, Rosa. But they're gone now. The house is mine. And so is the truth."

Rosa nods, then lowers her voice. "Miss Flossie changed after she found out about your father's affair. She put on a good show in public, but behind closed doors, she was a broken woman—mean and spiteful. She never let your daddy forget his mistake." She pauses, folding her napkin with slow, deliberate care. "She could see how much he adored Alice. Keeping that child out of your home was her revenge. She knew it would break his heart. And it did."

A young couple enters the bakery, hand in hand, eyes only for each other. I watch them for a moment before turning back to Rosa.

"Flossie was never openly cruel to Dad—not in front of me. But those last years before Dad got sick, I sensed something off between them. Now I understand." I pause, the truth settling in. "She never would've left him—the shame of divorce was unthinkable—but staying must've cost her just as much."

"They both paid for his sins in different ways. But Alice paid the most." Rosa shakes her head slowly, the weight of it all etched in her expression. "Your father wore his pain on his sleeve. He ached for his child. Keeping her at Waverly was the hardest thing he ever did." She pauses, her voice thickening. "He visited her every single week. And when he became too sick to go, he paid me to take his place. I never missed a week, Selwyn. Not once in all these years."

I swallow hard. "So, you had the opportunity to get to know Alice."

Rosa nods, eyes soft. "I know that child inside and out. And I love her with all my heart. As much as I love you. When Miss Flossie passed, I saw no reason for Alice to stay at Waverly. I believe you two belong together."

I glance down at my hands. "If that's so, why did Dad appoint Walter her legal guardian? He wanted her to stay at Waverly. How can I possibly go against his wishes?"

Rosa lifts a finger. "He was protecting her—making certain she was safe and provided for. But things changed. Your father had no way of knowing your mother would fall ill so soon after his death." She leans in slightly. "I did what I thought was right—what I truly believed he would've wanted, if he'd known the whole story. So, I took a chance on bringing her to Oxford. Maybe I went about it all wrong, but it was the only way I knew how." Her voice softens. "So no, Miss Selwyn. I didn't betray you. I tried to honor you. Both of you."

"Since you know Alice so well, you're the best person to

make this judgment. Do you think she can handle living in the real world?"

Rosa gives her head a vigorous nod. "Not only would she be safe, she'd be loved. Living a quiet, sheltered life here, with both of us looking out for her? I believe with all my heart she'd thrive. I've already seen it, even in the short time she stayed in the garage apartment."

I sit back in my chair, arms folded, mind deep in thought. Maybe Rosa's right. Maybe it's not about whether Alice can live in the real world but whether I can let her into mine.

"This is a big step, Rosa. I need to give it some more thought. But either way, will you please come back to work? I can't do life without you. And if I decide to bring Alice to live with me, I'll especially need your help."

Rosa appears surprised. "Wait. Did you fire me? Because I don't remember packing up my Tupperware."

I laugh, a real one this time, the first in what feels like forever.

As it fades, I glance across the table at her, feeling the familiar sting of tears. I've lost so many people and parts of myself along the way. But Rosa's still here. And Blossom, for a little while longer. In my house full of ghosts, that might just be enough to feel like home again.

Twenty-Seven

Later that afternoon, I'm standing at the fountain in the garden, Flossie's purple cremation jug tucked under my arm, when Griffin pulls into the driveway. He gets out and strolls over, hands in his pockets like he's just passing through.

"Hey, Selwyn. What're you up to?"

I don't turn to face him. "I could ask you the same question," I say to the garden. "I thought you were in Atlanta."

"I came back early."

I let out a dry humph. "I didn't think you were coming back at all."

"I hired a mediator to help Eleanor and I sort things out. Best money I've ever spent." He gives a low snort. "I'll admit, watching her beg for another chance was satisfying. Even more so when I turned her down. If that makes me an evil person, so be it. After everything she put me through . . . Well, I'm just relieved our marriage is finally over."

"Until the next time she uses your daughters to manipulate you into getting her way," I say, my eyes tracking a hummingbird hovering in front of the roses. Its wings blur, frantic and fragile, a flash of green and gold in the afternoon sun. "You always think it'll be different. That this time, she'll finally mean what she says. But people like Eleanor don't change. They just get better at dressing up the same old tactics."

"I don't think so, Selwyn. I don't love her anymore. Maybe I never really did. I was in love with the idea of her, not the person." He pauses, then adds, "The mediator helped convince Eleanor that the girls need more time with me. I now have them every other weekend. It'll mean a lot of driving back and forth, but I don't mind."

"Good for you," I mutter, keeping my eyes on the hummingbird.

He studies me for a beat. "You're in a mood. What's going on? And what's that thing you're holding?"

"Flossie. What's left of her anyway." I glance down at the urn in my arms. "I'm thinking of selling the house. I figured I leave her with it."

Griffin's brow furrows as he steps closer. "Why would you sell the house?" He turns me to face him, his expression softening. "What's wrong, Selwyn? You're scaring me."

I look away, focusing on a hummingbird darting near the roses, wings whirring like a heartbeat I can't quite calm. "A lot happened in the short time you were gone."

"Do you want to tell me about it?"

I let out a breath I didn't know I was holding. "Might as well. Let's go sit on the porch."

But when I turn toward the house, my foot sinks into the gravel path. I stumble, nearly dropping the urn. Griffin's hand darts out to steady me.

"Careful. Are you okay?"

I straighten, brushing off my arm even though there's no dirt. "Yes. I'm fine. Just off-balance lately."

Not just physically. Emotionally. Spiritually. Everything

feels shaky, like I've been standing still too long and the earth keeps shifting beneath me.

Griffin doesn't push. He just falls in step beside me as we make our way to the porch, the silence between us stretching but not straining. I clutch Flossie's urn a little tighter, wondering if I'm really ready to let go of the house—or if I'm just tired of holding on to all the hurt that lives inside it.

Up at the house, I set the urn gently on the porch floor, out of the way, and we settle onto the swing. Griffin nudges it into motion, the soft creak of the chains the only sound for a moment.

I walk him through the whirlwind of the past two days—finding out Alice is my half sister, the confrontation that led to her being sent back to Waverly, and my complete uncertainty over what to do next.

He leans back, absorbing it all. "Wow. All of that on top of Sadie taking off with the baby. You've really been through the wringer."

"Right?" I let out a dry laugh. "Feels like Sadie and Sam have been gone a month, not a few days."

Griffin rests his arm on the back of the swing. "You've had the weight of three lifetimes drop on you in two days. I understand why you feel conflicted."

I lean my head back against the swing, staring up at the ceiling. "I'm furious with my parents—for keeping Alice from me, for locking her away. Part of me wants to sell this house, put it all behind me, and get as far away from their ghosts as I can."

"And the other part?"

"Very much wants to take over Alice's legal guardianship. But the idea terrifies me. She has special needs. What if I can't meet them?"

Griffin doesn't hesitate. "I have complete faith in you, Selwyn. You will give that girl everything she needs. And if something comes up that's beyond your wheelhouse, you'll find the support she needs. You won't be alone in this."

I close my eyes, letting that sink in. "What scares me the most is the idea of forever. Or at least, my lifetime. I believe she's capable of living independently, maybe even having a career one day. But what if I'm wrong? What if she needs me for the rest of my life?"

He shifts slightly beside me. "So? Would that be such a bad thing?"

I open my eyes and lift my head. "No. But it's a huge commitment. And what if we don't get along? She wasn't here that long. What if there are things I don't know—issues I'm not prepared for?"

"You can *what if* yourself right out of this, Selwyn. But the bottom line is simple."

He waits until I meet his gaze. "Do you love Alice?"

I nod. "Very much."

"Then you'll overcome whatever hurdles you encounter. There are no guarantees in life. Parenthood doesn't come with a manual, and neither does being a sister—not under these circumstances. You'll learn as you go. You'll make mistakes, but you'll also make a difference." He gives a small, wry smile. "You don't need to have all the answers right now. You just need to show up. Love her. Listen to her. Let her know she matters. That alone is more than she's had her whole life."

"I don't know, Griffin. It seems easier to sell the house and start a new life in a different college town. Chapel Hill or Athens, Georgia."

"Where you know no one and have no connections," Griffin says.

"Exactly. I'll dedicate my life to my academia. Bury myself in syllabi and student essays."

"You're a Faulkner expert, Selwyn. They don't care about Faulkner at other schools. What would you even teach?"

"Faulkner doesn't define my career, Griffin. I teach other courses—literature, writing, Southern lit—"

Griffin tilts my chin toward him. "What's happened to you? The Selwyn I knew didn't run from hard things. She stood her ground. She fought back."

I pull away, my gaze drifting toward the garden. "That Selwyn doesn't exist anymore. Life beat her down."

"I don't believe that." His voice is steady. "You may be down, but you are *not* out. You're scared—understandably. But becoming Alice's legal guardian doesn't have to be the impossible burden you're building it up to be." He pauses, letting the weight of his words fill the space between us. "It's really very simple. Just show up. She's your sister. Your family. Why is there even a choice? Alice doesn't need flawless. She needs you."

"I've been so afraid of doing the wrong thing," I say quietly. "Of failing her. Of being one more person who lets her down." My voice catches, and I force myself to meet his gaze. "But maybe you're right. Maybe showing up is enough. Maybe that's where it starts."

The words settle between us, tentative but true. And for the first time, I let myself imagine what it might look like—not just to take Alice in but to build something real with her. A home. A future. A life stitched together, not from obligation but from choice.

I exhale slowly. "I don't know if I'll get it right, but I think I'm ready to try."

The sound of fingernails tapping marble echoes through the quiet house. I follow it to the kitchen and stop short. Blossom isn't at the stove, humming gospels and flipping eggs like she has every other morning since she arrived. Instead, she's seated at the counter, shoulders hunched, her tea untouched. She drums her fingers with a restless rhythm, eyes fixed on a spot only she can see.

I cross the threshold slowly. "Blossom?"

She doesn't glance up. Just keeps drumming. "I'm worried about you, Daisy. It's like I've been talking to a wall. I can't seem to reach you."

Before I can muster a response, the back door opens and Rosa steps inside, her face pale, lips pressed tight.

"What is it?" I ask. "You look like you've seen a ghost."

Rosa clutches a tissue and dabs at her eyes. "I just got off the phone with a friend at Waverly. She works in the cafeteria." Her voice breaks. "It's Alice. She's not doing well. She's not eating. Won't come out of her room. They say she's gone quiet —like she's shut the world out."

The thought of Alice—alone, unhappy, shut away—

cracks what's left of my heart. "That's it. I'm done." I grab my phone and scroll through my contacts.

"What're you doing?" Rosa asks.

"Calling Walter. He's still her legal guardian. He can authorize the transfer."

Rosa's face lights up, and Blossom presses a hand to her chest. "Praise the Lord."

Walter answers on the second ring, his voice gruff.

"Sorry to call so early," I begin, launching straight into it. "I want to petition the court for legal guardianship. But in the meantime, I need you to contact Waverly. Let them know I'm coming to bring Alice home. She's going to live with me."

There's a pause, then Walter's tone shifts—warmer, almost reverent. "You're doing the right thing, Selwyn. Your father would be proud."

"And my mother would kill me," I reply. "But honestly? I don't care. My gut tells me this is right."

"You have my full support. Anything you need, just ask."

I suddenly can't wait to get to my sister. "I appreciate that. You can start by telling Waverly I'm on my way. I should be there within the hour."

As I hang up, Blossom asks, "What about your class?"

"I'm canceling. My students will be thrilled," I say, already drafting the email, thumbs flying across my phone's screen.

I slip my phone in my pocket and square my shoulders. "Okay! Here I go. Wish me luck."

Rosa and Blossom exchange a look—silent but decided.

"No way are we letting you do this alone," Blossom says, scrambling to her feet. "We're coming with you."

A voice cuts in from the kitchen doorway. "Where are y'all going?"

We turn to see Griffin, holding a to-go cup of coffee and looking mildly suspicious.

"To get Alice," I say, grinning.

He raises his eyes to the ceiling. "Thanks be to God. I'm coming too."

Rosa frowns. "Can we all fit in one car?"

"Of course," I say, slinging my purse over my shoulder. "It'll be like the olden days—one of my many high school road trips to the beach."

Blossom pours to-go coffees for all of us, and we file out to my Land Cruiser. Jimmy Buffett blares from the speakers as we cruise down the highway, all of us singing at the tops of our lungs. I steal frequent glances at Griffin in the passenger seat beside me. He hasn't looked this carefree since we reconnected a few weeks ago.

As we near Waverly Hill, the laughter fades. I grow quiet, the weight of what's ahead settling in my chest like something too big to swallow. The road winds upward, and with every turn, my grip on the moment tightens.

Griffin reaches for my hand, giving it a firm squeeze. He doesn't let go. "You're not regretting this, are you?"

"Not for a second. I'm just afraid Alice will be mad at me for not coming sooner."

He lets out a soft laugh. "Alice? I'm not even sure she knows how to be mad."

And he's right. She's waiting on the front steps of the enormous brick building, her belongings in mismatched bags and boxes at her feet. The moment she sees us, she leaps up and throws her arms around me.

"What took you so long?" she asks, beaming.

Then she hugs everyone in turn, like we're the guests of honor at a welcome-home parade. "Let's go. I can't wait to get home."

She insists on sitting in the back between Blossom and Rosa because, as she puts it, "Griffin's a man, so he should definitely ride shotgun." She doesn't stop talking the entire drive.

I'm worried she'll want to stay in the garage again. I'd much rather have her in the house, where I can keep a closer eye on her. Meeting her gaze in the rearview mirror, I say, "Alice, how do you feel about living in the house with me? You can have Sadie's old room—my childhood bedroom. We can fix it up however you'd like."

She nearly comes off the seat. "Do you mean it? Can I really stay in the house? Like I'm one of the family?"

My heart shatters and swells at once. I choke back a sob. "We are family, Alice. We're sisters."

"Can I paint my room lavender? It's my favorite color."

I smile at her in the mirror. "Of course. Lavender is a lovely color. It suits you."

"Can I go to college like you said?" she asks eagerly.

I return my attention to the road. "I haven't looked into it yet, but I'm sure it won't be a problem. We'll take the summer off, get to know each other better, and then you can start in the fall."

"Yippee," she squeals, doing a seated version of a victory dance.

We order pizza for lunch and crowd around the kitchen table, laughing and talking over each other like we've done it a hundred times before. Afterward, Griffin heads out to show a house, leaving Alice and me to spend the afternoon settling her into her room, while Rosa and Blossom take over the kitchen, filling the house with the comforting smells of her homecoming dinner.

The menu includes chicken nuggets—crispy, not soggy— because Rosa insists on baking them just right. Macaroni and cheese, but only the orange kind with spiral noodles will do. Sliced strawberries and mini marshmallows, served in the same bowl. Pickles on the side, because "they go with everything" according to Alice. Extra crispy waffle fries served with ketchup and ranch—mixed together, of course. And for dessert: brownies with rainbow sprinkles. Alice says sprinkles make them taste better.

We're gathering in the kitchen at six thirty when Griffin walks in. Rosa and Blossom quietly slip out, and that's when I notice there are only three place settings at the table.

They're matchmaking again, I think to myself. But I don't mind. Griffin, Alice, and I already feel like a family.

After dinner, Griffin helps me with the dishes while Alice lingers at the counter, thumbing through her phone. The kitchen hums with quiet contentment—the kind that only comes after a shared meal and a hard-won sense of peace.

Then Alice lets out a sharp gasp.

I spin around. "What is it?"

Her eyes are wide, glued to the screen. "It's Sadie. She posted while we were eating. She looks horrible."

I come around the counter and peer over her shoulder at the phone. The photograph is blurry, a filtered selfie taken in dim light—maybe in front of a mirror. Her mascara is slightly smudged. Her smile doesn't quite reach her eyes. In the background, barely visible, is the baby's playpen.

The caption reads: *Some days, it feels like I'm watching my life happen from underwater. I smile. I function. But none of this feels like me.*

Alice pinches the screen, zooming in on Sadie's selfie. "There's Sam," she says, pointing to the playpen.

I look closer. There he is, red-faced with mouth wide open, brows furrowed, arms flailing in the air. I can almost hear the wail through the still image.

Sadie, meanwhile, is locked on the camera, a hollow half smile on her face, her eyes rimmed in smeared eyeliner. It's like she doesn't even notice him.

A chill slides down my spine. "He's crying, and she's taking selfies?"

Griffin leans over my shoulder. "That's not just tired, new-mom stuff. Something's off."

Alice clicks on Sadie's profile and scrolls through the recent posts. "She's been sharing stuff like that for days. But not as bad as this. This is *really* bad."

As we're staring at the screen, a new post appears. A photo of a half-packed duffel bag lying open on the bed. A baby bottle is tipped on its side nearby, a pacifier half-hidden under the edge of a blanket. An open journal rests beside it, pages curling at the corners. The lighting is harsh, unfiltered, and unforgiving.

The caption: *I'm tired of pretending I'm okay. This isn't the life I wanted. I don't know how to fix it. I just want out.*

I let out a low whistle. "That is a cry for help if I've ever seen one. We have to do something."

"We need to take Sam away from her," Alice says, jaw set. "She doesn't deserve to have him if she can't take care of him."

I smooth back my sister's hair. "We can't just take him away from her, Alice. She's his mother. But I agree, we need to find her, to offer our help. Do we have any idea where she might be?"

"I do." Alice scrolls quickly. "She left breadcrumbs for us, like Hansel and Gretel."

"Let me see that," Griffin says, taking the phone from her. As he drags his finger down the screen, photos appear. A *Welcome to Gulf Shores* sign. A dingy apartment complex called *Pelican Court*. A weathered door with the numbers 305 painted in red—blood red. A bad omen, I think.

"She's leading us right to her," Alice says, her crystal eyes wide. "She's begging us to come. We have to go."

My mouth drops open. "To Gulf Shores? That's seven hours away. I have my last class tomorrow. I've already missed two this week."

"Can't you get someone to cover for you?" Griffin asks, handing Alice back her phone.

"Griffin's right, Selwyn. We have to go," Alice pleads.

He points at the phone. "That young woman is desperate."

"Which means Sam might be in danger," Alice adds. "He belongs here with us, Selwyn. You should be his mama."

I gulp. "This is a huge step. I'm not sure I'm ready for a baby."

"Sure, you are," Alice says brightly. "You and Griffin can get married. He's always wanted to be a boy dad."

Griffin burst out laughing.

"Did you tell her that?" I ask, raising an eyebrow.

He shakes his head, grinning. "Selwyn, honey, you were born ready for a baby. But no one says you have to keep it. There are other options."

"Right," Alice says, nodding earnestly. "Maybe Sadie can come back here. She can live with us until she figures things out. She can have her room back."

I smile at my sister. "No way! That room is yours now. Sadie can have the guest room." I return to the sink. "But you're right. There are other options. Maybe Sadie wants to put the baby up for adoption. We can help with that."

"Exactly," Griffin says. "We'll figure all that out in due time. But for now—"

I cut him off with a breathy sigh. "All right. I'll email a colleague and ask her to cover my last class. I already have the lecture ready."

"Yes!" Alice whispers loudly. "Can we leave tonight?"

Griffin looks at me expectantly.

"Let's wait until tomorrow," I say. "We'll leave at first light. We should probably pack a bag in case we have to spend the night."

"Probably be a good idea," Griffin says. "We'll take my Tahoe."

I glance up at him while rinsing the last plate. "You don't trust Bluebell?"

Alice answers before he can. "It's not that. We can't make a seven-hour trip without modern conveniences like Apple CarPlay."

"What's Apple CarPlay?" I tease, and we all laugh.

"I'll finish up here. Alice, run upstairs, pack your bag, and get ready for bed." I slide the plate in the dishwasher and turn to face Griffin. "And you need to get some sleep too."

He nods. "Agreed. And I want to stop on the way home for gas."

I walk him to the door and pull him into a hug. "You're a good man, Griffin."

"I wasn't always, Selwyn. At least not to you. I'm trying to make it up to you."

"You're doing a good job of it. Thank you—for your help with Alice. And with this. It's a lot. Most men couldn't handle it."

He smiles softly. "I'm not most men."

I stand in the doorway and watch as he backs out of the driveway. Then I turn back to the kitchen, slowly putting away leftovers, my mind a million miles away.

A voice startles me from behind. "Don't second-guess yourself, Daisy. You're doing the right thing. This path chose you, sweetheart. And you've got more grit and grace in you than you realize. You don't have to have it all figured out. Your heart is in the right place, and that's all that matters."

I don't admonish her for eavesdropping or ask how she knows. I'm just relieved I don't have to explain. "I'm scared to death, Blossom. But I have faith that with Griffin and Alice by my side, we'll do right by Sadie." I lean in close to her, breathing in her floral scent. Roses, I think. "You'll be here when we get back, right? I'm going to need my spiritual advisor to guide me."

She wraps her arms around me. "Yes, Daisy. I'll be here when you get back. But I will see you before you leave in the morning."

The morning. Tomorrow.

I have no idea what we're walking into. But for the first time in a long time, I won't be walking alone.

Blossom sees us off at dawn with foil-wrapped sausage biscuits and a large Thermos of coffee.

Taking a seven-hour car trip is one way to get to know someone. And Alice is determined to tell us every single thing about her life. I give Griffin credit—whether or not he's actually listening, he at least appears interested.

My stomach knots as we pass the *Welcome to Gulf Shores* sign from Sadie's photo. We've driven seven hours. There's no turning back now.

The apartment complex—Pelican Court—is dingier in person, if that's even possible. The paint is peeling, the shutters hang crooked, and the landscaping consists of a cracked sidewalk and one dying palm tree.

We climb three flights of rusted metal stairs, the railings sticky with humidity. As we approach apartment 305, we hear raised voices—two adults arguing—and the unmistakable, high-pitched wail of a baby.

When Griffin knocks on the door, the arguing stops, but the crying doesn't.

I elbow him aside and pound on the door. "Sadie! It's Selwyn."

A muffled voice calls back. "Go away, Selwyn. I don't want you here."

Something crashes inside, and I knock louder. "Open up, Sadie! We're not leaving. If you don't let us in, I'm calling the police."

The door swings open. A disheveled young man—jaw tight, shirt stained—glares at me. Presumably Jake.

"What do you want?" he asks flatly.

"To see Sadie," I blurt.

He jerks his chin toward the sofa. "There she is. Now you've seen her, you can leave."

Sadie is curled up under a blanket, her face barely visible. Alice gasps and rushes over to her, tugging the blanket away from her face to reveal a black eye and busted lip.

Spinning around, Alice lunges at Jake, pounding his chest with her fists. "What's wrong with you? Don't you know you're not supposed to hit girls?"

Griffin pulls her back gently. "Let me handle this, Alice."

Then, he grabs a fistful of Jake's shirt and slams him against the wall. "Did you hear her? Didn't your parents teach you not to hit girls?"

Sadie scrambles up, clutching her blanket. "Please, Griffin. Let him go. He's not worth it. I'm leaving him as soon as I figure out what to do with the baby. I'm not ready to be a parent. I can't support myself, let alone a baby. This isn't the life I want." She turns to me, eyes pleading. "Will you take him? Please?"

Griffin turns back to Jake. "Are you willing to give up your parental rights?"

He snorts. "Are you kidding me? This has been a nightmare. I don't want a kid." He sweeps an arm at Sadie. "And I sure as hell don't want her as my wife."

Sadie glares at him. "The feeling's mutual. Jerk."

Griffin shoves him toward the door. "Get out! Before I call the cops."

Jake bolts, slamming the door behind him.

"Please, Selwyn! Say you'll take him," Sadie says, her voice trembling.

A wave of panic tightens around my chest. "I can't," I whisper. "What if you change your mind? What if you later decide you want him back? I'm not sure I could give him up again."

She shakes her head. "I won't. I've tried, but I don't feel anything for him. I haven't even named him yet." Tears stream down her face. "I'm a horrible person. Broken. Like who doesn't love their own child?"

I dig in my purse for a tissue, gently blotting away her tears. "You're not broken, Sadie. Love doesn't always rush in all at once. Sometimes the deepest love is in making the hardest choice—and being brave enough to let go."

Sadie clutches the blanket tighter around her, but she doesn't look away. In the smallest voice, she says, "I really do want you to have him. I think I always did."

I hesitate. "Have you even considered your other options? A reputable adoption agency could place him with a family— maybe younger parents, if that's what you want."

"You're not that old, Selwyn." A hint of a smile tugs at her lips. "It was meant to be—me ending up in your class. I can give you the baby you've always wanted. And you, in turn, can give me freedom. Peace of mind. Just knowing he's being well taken care of."

"Why don't you come back to Oxford with us?" I suggest. "You won't have to see the baby if you don't want. You can live in the garage apartment. Give yourself a little more time. Until you're certain."

"I'm certain, Selwyn." Her voice doesn't waver. "I can't go

back to Oxford. I know myself—at least I know the Sadie I was before I got myself into this mess. It's better if I just walk away."

I glance over at Alice, who is changing the baby's diaper and dressing him in clean clothes. "You're coming home to live with us," she coos softly.

Sadie's lips part in a sad smile. "You've got yourself a helper."

"Apparently so."

It's all so sudden. So forever. But when Alice places the baby in my arms, the world narrows to just the two of us. The noise, the clutter, the doubt—it all fades. His tiny body is warm against my chest, his breath soft and rhythmic, his presence so small and yet somehow overwhelming. And I know. I know in the deepest part of me—he is meant to be mine. *Sam.*

Griffin touches my elbow. "Selwyn? What're you thinking?"

I nod, unable to speak for fear of breaking down.

He turns to Sadie. "Are you willing to sign a form, giving Selwyn temporary guardianship until the formal adoption can take place?"

"Yes! Let's get this show on the road. I want to get out of here before Jake comes back."

I frown. "Where will you go?"

"A friend offered me a place until I get a job. She refused to help me when I had the baby. But she'll help me now."

"Some friend," Griffin mutters.

"I know. She's trying to be helpful in her own way." Sadie places a hand on her now-flat belly. "In hindsight, I didn't go through with the pregnancy because I wanted a baby. I just couldn't bring myself to have an abortion. I was so focused on getting my diploma, I never stopped to think about what my life would look like after he was born. Babies are a lot of work." She kisses the baby's head. "You're in good hands now, little one."

"This is for you," Griffin says, handing her an envelope.

Her eyes widen as she opens it. "There must be a thousand dollars in here."

Griffin blushes. "I figured you'll need something to live on until you find a job."

She clutches the envelope to her chest. "I don't know what to say. Thank you. You've both been so kind to me. I don't deserve it."

"You most certainly do," I tell her. "And never let anyone tell you otherwise."

"Ready to go!" Alice announces, the baby's gear packed in a hodgepodge of tote bags at her feet.

"Aren't you efficient?" Sadie says without the sarcasm she had a few days ago.

"We have a long drive ahead of us. When's the last time he ate? Is he on any kind of schedule?" Alice asks, sounding more like a grown-up with every word.

"I fed him about an hour ago," Sadie says. "No schedule—I've been feeding him whenever he cries."

"Well, we'll have to fix that," Alice says, breaking the tension.

Our laughter rings hollow, too light for the weight of the moment.

We say our goodbyes in a tangle of hugs and half-hearted smiles. Sadie holds the baby one last time, pressing a kiss to his forehead before placing him gently in my arms. No promises are made. We all know this needs to be a clean break.

Alice insists on sitting in the back with the baby, her arms curled around him like she's afraid to let him go. The baby cries halfway through Alabama. When we stop for gas just outside Montgomery, Alice unbuckles him from his car seat, cooing and rocking until he quiets. She feeds him on a splintered bench in the shade while Griffin fills the tank, and I watch them both from a few steps away, like I've slipped out of my own body and into someone else's life—still trying to absorb everything we've just done.

We stop again two hours later, this time for ourselves. A roadside diner with sticky booths and terrible coffee—but the biscuits are hot and buttery, and Alice polishes off a second one with jam. Griffin asks how I'm holding up. I tell him I'm okay. I'm not. But I will be.

It's nearly dark. Alice and the baby are both sound asleep in the back seat when Griffin reaches for my hand. "What Alice said last night was spot on," he says, quietly. "I've always wanted a son. I was desperate to try for a third child, but Eleanor wasn't interested."

He glances over at me. "When the dust settles, I'm going to ask you to marry me. If you say no, I'll keep asking until you say yes. Because I can see into your soul, Selwyn Aldridge, and I know you want the same thing I do—to raise this quirky little family together."

I smile over at him. "I won't say *no* when you ask me the first time. Because I can see into your soul, Griffin McRae. And I can feel how much you love me—and our two new children."

I rest my head against the window, Griffin's hand still wrapped in mine. The road hums beneath us, steady and sure, stretching out like a promise. For the first time in a long time, the future doesn't scare me. It feels real. Tangible. Like something I can finally reach for without losing myself in the process.

Thirty

To my surprise, we settle into our new lives in the blue Victorian on Willow Way with ease. Alice reads every book she can find on infant care. Within days, she's whipped Sam's feeding schedule into shape, and he's sleeping for long stretches at night. I warn her repeatedly not to dote on him, but she can't seem to help herself.

With Walter's help, I begin the process of becoming Alice's legal guardian and adopting the baby—my son. Together, Alice, Griffin, and I agree on the name Samuel Eli Aldridge. But we'll keep calling him Sam.

"You need something else to occupy your time," I say to Alice one night over dinner. "You're a gifted writer with a vivid imagination. Have you ever considered a publishing career? You could write thrillers. Or, since you love children so much, maybe a series for kids or young adults."

"I already told you, Selwyn. I want to be a forensic accountant."

"Oh?" I say with a raised eyebrow. "You were serious about that?"

She gives me a look. "Of course I was."

I nod, impressed. "Well. I stand corrected."

"I excel at math, Selwyn." She shovels in a mouthful of rice and sets down her fork. "I have it all figured out. I'll get my undergraduate degree in accounting from Ole Miss, followed by my Master of Accountancy. Then I'll sit for the CPA exam. After that, I'll earn my CFE—Certified Fraud Examiner. Then I'm going to apply for a job with the FBI. Organized crime, financial fraud, cybercrime, embezzlement, terrorism financing—you name it."

I can no longer hold back my smile. "I see you've given this a lot of thought."

She has. More than I realized. And working for the FBI means she'll be moving away from Oxford—far away—but that's years down the road. Still, the thought settles like a pebble in my chest.

I'll lose her. But that's what parents do. We raise them to grow wings, knowing full well they'll fly straight out of our arms. All we can hope is that they remember where home is, and who helped them soar.

"Based on my calculations, I can do it in five years," Alice continues. "Three years for my bachelor's, one for my master's and the CPA, and six months to pass the CFE."

"I guess we need to work on getting you into college."

Alice's face lights up. "Yes! Please!"

And so, I confer with a colleague in the business school, who agrees to administer a series of mathematical aptitude tests. No one is surprised when she scores at a genius level. Alice is beside herself when the college accepts her into the freshman class starting this fall.

One month after we bring Sam home, I decide it's time to scatter Flossie's ashes. It's something I always imagined doing alone, but now, it doesn't seem right without Blossom.

We gather in the garden by the fountain. Blossom wears a

floral dress with a wreath of roses in her hair, like a benediction of summer. I don Flossie's gardening hat and her worn muck boots, an odd sort of armor for the task ahead. We stand in silence for a minute, each lost in our own thoughts.

For the past six years, I've taken care of my dying parents. Now, I'm caring for a newborn and a young woman still finding her way. Even though Alice is technically my sister, I feel like she's mine to look after—like a daughter. Turns out taking care of people *is* my thing. Not only what I'm meant to do but what I want to do.

As I move slowly through the garden, scattering ashes into the breeze, I feel the tension begin to lift—the old weight of perfection Flossie carried and passed down to me. The pressure to always look right, act right, be the version of myself she wanted to show the world. With each step, each release of gray dust into the flowerbeds and soil, I let go of her expectations. I let go of needing her approval.

When I reach the old hydrangea bush—the one that always bloomed best under Flossie's care—I pause.

"I tried," I whisper. "Lord knows, I tried to be who you wanted me to be. But I finally figured out how to be who *I* need to be." I tilt the last of the ashes into the soil. "Maybe one day you'll approve. In the meantime . . . this is goodbye."

Blossom steps beside me, her voice soft and sure. "I've watched you grow since the day I arrived, Daisy. Into yourself. Into your calling. Into love. Flossie may not have known how to show it, but I believe she was proud in her own way. And if she could see you now—choosing family, choosing peace, becoming your own person, she'd be proud all over again."

I nod, tears stinging but not falling. I feel lighter. Rooted. Ready.

"You're leaving soon." I know the time is coming. I wish she could stay here forever, but others need her more than me.

As though reading my mind, she says, "You don't need

me. You've got Griffin." She nods at the sparkling solitaire diamond on my finger. "Solid as a rock, that one. When did he propose?"

"Last night after supper." I hold my hand out, admiring the ring. "On the bench swing. Nothing fancy needed. Just his promise to love, honor, and cherish the rest of our days."

Letting my hand drop, I smile over at Blossom. "How will I reach you if I need you? Will you share your contact info?"

"Ha! I don't have a number, Daisy." She flashes her cell phone. "This is just for information purposes. If you ever need me, wish upon a star, and I'll come running."

I give her the purple urn. "Please take this with you. I don't need to hold on to it anymore."

Blossom accepts it with a soft smile. "Then you've already let her go."

I blink fast, willing my tears to leave. "You've changed my life, Blossom."

She leans in and touches my cheek. "No, sweetheart. You changed it yourself. I just came to remind you who you are."

A breeze stirs the hem of her dress, carrying the faint scent of roses and warm earth.

I catch a flicker in my bedroom window. Alice and the baby are there, waving down at us.

When I turn back toward her, Blossom is gone—vanished. Behind me, her minibus has disappeared. In its place sits the purple urn, now filled with a large bouquet of daisies.

Leaning against the urn is an envelope with a handwritten note.

You said goodbye with grace. Now, say hello with open arms. One life released, another just begun. Love well, Daisy. —Blossom

· · ·

I press the note to my heart and smile. Some people walk into your life. Blossom appeared like a prayer—and left like a blessing. And now it's my turn to carry the light forward.

About the Author

Ashley Farley writes heartfelt stories about women navigating life's challenges. Her characters are mothers, daughters, sisters, and wives facing real-life struggles with resilience and grace. Best known for her Sweeney Sisters series, Ashley's books have touched the hearts of readers far and wide.

A wife and mother of two young adults, for more than two decades, Ashley has split her time between Richmond and the Northern Neck of Virginia. Yet, a piece of her heart will always belong to the South Carolina Lowcountry, where she draws inspiration from the moss-draped oaks, coastal cuisine, and the warm, welcoming spirit of its people.

Ashley loves to hear from her readers. Visit her website @ ashleyfarley.com or online bookstore @ ashleyfarleybook-s.com. Get free exclusive content by signing up for her newsletter @ ashleyfarley.com/newsletter-signup/

9 781956 684728